AF260930

Darker Shade of Pale

Her Escape, Her Freedom

First Edition: August 2013
Printed in the United States of America
ISBN: 978-1490956596

This novel was originally published online as INTERVENTION OF ANA.

Darker Shade of Pale

Her Escape, Her Freedom

by
Mandi Rei Serra

PART ONE

HER ESCAPE

Chapter One

"Selesta," my husband called from the bedroom. "I want to talk." His voice gave no option but to do as requested or face the consequences of independence.

Immediately, the muscles in my legs felt leaden, heavy. My shoulders tensed, and my breathing quickened. Those words of his, while spoken kindly, didn't do much to allay the whirlwind of thought my mind unleashed. Maybe I'm wrong, and Jakob Christos Haytham, brilliant scientist that he was, truly wasn't an abusive husband.

The hickies he gave me in retaliation for going out with an old friend and wearing something that hinted at cleavage, that's not abuse. Not like I got socked in the mouth for lipping off again.

I sighed. When I agreed to marry him, I didn't sign up for the emotional roller-coaster that seems second nature to his personality. How did he hide it for so long?

"Coming, Christos." Sometimes I wished he'd relax enough to be called Chris, and not by his middle name. Such a mouthful, sometimes. If he can call me Selli, why can I not call him by a shortened name? Sigh. I left the bathroom after splashing cold water on my face, and walked to him with my head bowed down. He always was nicer when I seemed sorry for causing him to hurt me.

When I reached him, I fell to my knees and said, "Forgive me for provoking you, my husband and master." Sickened me to say that. Every time I die a little more inside. Our wedding night was the first time he instructed me in the manner befitting his wife. Stupid, naive dolt that I was, believed him. Took it to heart after he hit me.

Christos lifted my chin and looked in my eyes. "Ah, my beautiful, sweet, brave girl. I'm sorry I did that," as he spoke, he let his fingers drift over the red marks on my neck. "But when I tell you how things are, the matter is done for discussion. No arguments. You should know better by now."

I tried not to heave an impatient sigh. "All I wanted to do is hit the mall, like I used to. Personal shoppers are swell and all, but sometimes a girl wants to get hands-on in the bargain bin." Sometimes, levity works on him. If I could keep him from getting angry, then I don't have to worry about his reactions.

"You are my wife now, Selli. You can't expect to live an out-moded life of an average person. That's not you. Three years ago, before we got married, sure. But you're better than that now."

My eyebrows danced a moment as I tried to wrap my mind around his statement. "When malls no longer exist is when I'll consider them outmoded. What's so wrong with me choosing my own clothes and getting some me time?" He fell in love with me, being an average person. Now that's not okay? I resented the sensation of being a dog on a leash, although no physical barrier really held me back. Just the menace emanating from Christos' gaze kept me in check.

"You don't have to make those choices, Selli. You're beyond that. You're mine and I'll take care of you in every way. You don't need *you* time, you need *us* time."

"That's sweet, Christos." *And stifling.* I put my hand on his arm and looked up into that statuesque face. "Can't I go incognito and pretend to be one of the plebeians? A non-Halloween Halloween?"

"No sexy costumes." Christos cracked a small smile, which fed the fires of my hope. An idea came to me. Dare I be so bold as to ask such a thing from my husband? Would he agree? There was but only one way to find out.

I was about to bite my lip in vexation when inspiration came. "I was wondering if we could acquire a female bodyguard, so I could go shopping myself and you won't have to worry about little ol' me." I waited on bated breath for his reply.

Slowly, Christos began to nod. "I like that idea. It will free Morgan up for other things. I'd hate for him to follow you into a department store changing room to make sure you're safe."

I tried to hide my giddiness. "May I interview the applicants? Privately?" If I can ask them questions, maybe I can find one whose loyalty will be mine, not Christos'. I need someone I can trust, someone who isn't already a part of Christos' minions and informants.

"Why *privately*?" The tone of Christos' voice deepened grew serious. I quelled at the thought of him getting wind of my plan.

"Girl talk. Periods, blood clots, bloating, stuff like that. And when I say blood clots, I mean the type that stick to maxi pads, not the type Morgan gets when he takes a bullet. PMS, PMDD, PTSD, you know, just girl stuff. Unless you want to discuss the benefits of Tampax over Kotex?"

Christos' look of disgust spelled out his feelings. He wouldn't wish tampon talk on another male. "Sounds fair."

I smirked on the inside. Men generally hate chunky lady-bits blood.

"So I can have a bodyguard for my very own?" Batted my eyes and plead as sweetly as I could. Hated it. Hated acting and pretending just to get my way. If I asked for one, I'd be flat-out denied. He liked me being coy.

"Yes, and only the best for you. You are like a beautiful jewel which must be guarded, cherished." He slid a hand down my cheek and I tried not to wince. Too many times that hand delivered a stinging blow.

"I just want to be me, Christos. Inept, clumsy, me." I took a step away from the power emanating from my husband, for a breather. Whenever he neared, I can't think. Part of me goes stupid because the man looks like a statue, perfect in every proportion. The other part gets freaked, because Christos doesn't like people not going along with his decrees. A part of me missed hanging out with Kate in out apartment, cramming for finals.

The stress of testing goes away. Not so much when it comes to Christos.

"You aren't inept, except when you don't listen to me. Then I have to make you listen." He gave a small smile to soften the blow. 'Making me listen' usually involves him grabbing an arm and getting in my face.

I suppressed my frown. "Could I go shopping with Morgan to pick up some turtlenecks? I don't have any scarves to cover this." Let Christos take another look at the fingers marks he left on me. Let him see what his anger did.

He didn't bother to look. "Yes, take Morgan. He drives, though."

"Why did you buy me a car you won't let me drive?"

"Because you are mine. Body and soul. I will never let you go, Selli. I never give up on that which I consider mine. But you knew that when you married, me didn't you? Of course you did."

My heart sank. To be loved is a wonderful thing. But people need space to breathe. I feel like I'm gasping at the last lungful of oxygen before drowning in a swamp of total control.

Chapter Two

"Hi, I'm Zamara Malone."

Applicant number 15 to be interviewed. A part of the bargain struck between my husband and I was that the responsibility of finding and hiring a female "companion" fell on my shoulders. I'm okay with that, in fact, thrilled about it. When Morgan and I went shopping, I asked him what he considered the top three agencies. He replied. I researched, called and filtered through hundreds of resumes and dossiers to find those I considered compatible for my needs. I suspected many applicants would be plants-- no telling how far Christos would go to keep me under his thumb.

I stood and held my hand out to shake Zamara's. "Pleased to meet you. I am Selesta Haytham. Please, have a seat." I gestured to the chair on the other side of the small hotel room table. I didn't want to have the interviews where Christos could overhear or where I'd have to worry about his informants. He's under the assumption that I'm using the hotel's smaller conference room to conduct my interviews. I'm thankful that Christos' new project started, freeing him from insisting on participating in the interviewing process. For a while there, I was scared he'd try to work himself into my endeavor at the last minute. Luckily that didn't happen.

Zamara sat down, put her briefcase next to the chair then placed hands on her lap and looked expectantly in my direction. Masses of black curls were pulled back from her face, displaying a delicate bone structure housing intelligent blue eyes. I requested applicants wear business casual, as I felt it set the tone on a couple levels. First off, I want to blend in again. I don't want to be a sculpture on a pedestal- I'd rather be in the mass of people looking somewhere else. Secondly, I miss relaxing. Hard to do that when one is surrounded by suits all the time. Zamara wore a pale blue cowl-necked cashmere sweater and a pleated wool skirt, the color of a ripe acorn. Black pumps. She fit the definition of business casual by my standard.

I had a good feeling about Ms. Malone. According to the dossier provided by Xerxes Inc, Zamara Marion Malone, born of Irish and Bedouin parents. Marine Corps vet, ex-FBI, ties to CIA. Specialist in hand-to-hand combat and survivalist tactics. Proficient in firearms, but her preferred weapon was the KA-BAR - Marine Corps issue knife/bayonet. As I spoke to her, I found Zamara's personality to be competent, quiet, and whimsical at times.

We indulged in idle chatter for a bit before I got down to business. "To help determine compatibility, I like to ask questions about certain topics. There is no right or wrong answer, as it's more of an opinion I'm seeking."

"Fair enough."

I smiled. "Do you have any charities you favor?"

"I volunteer twice a week at the MidTown Women's Shelter. Used to volunteer at the Humane Society, but then I developed an allergic reaction to animal dander, so that put the kibosh on me playing with the fuzzies."

The dossier mentioned the women's shelter; one of the reasons I looked forward to meeting Zamara. "Why did you start bodyguarding? You have a very impressive resume, Ms. Malone."

"I found I can't save the entire world by myself. I'll settle for saving the world one person at a time." She smiled. "That, and more often than not, it's more realistic to accomplish."

"Why did you leave the FBI?"

The smile faded, to be replaced with a business-like demeanor. "Protocol has its use. However, I do not believe in hiding behind protocol to get things accomplished. Sometimes protocol wastes valuable time and lives."

I nodded. Sometimes, time is of the essence in life. I decided to ask the really important questions. "When hired, who has your loyalty- your primary or the one signing your paycheck?"

Immediately she replied, "My primary, of course. Money corrupts, it's a fact."

She got a bonus point. "Would you be willing to teach me self-defense?"

"If you wanted, sure. It's a skill every woman should learn."

Another bonus point. "I see you are a survivalist tactic specialist. What does that entail, exactly?"

"Living off the land when one has limited or no resources."

I smiled wide. The plan was coming alive.

"I think I like what I see when it comes to you, Ms Malone. If offered the position immediately, would you accept?"

"Certainly."

"Consider yourself hired. My husband's people will send over the paperwork for you to complete."

Zamara smiled wide, and for a moment I was blinded by the happiness on her face. "Wonderful! I look forward to working with you."

"Not as much as I do, I'm pretty sure of that. I'd like to discuss your primary objective."

"You are not my primary?"

"I am, but not in the way you think." My cell phone began ringing. I saw that it was Christos and stifled a sigh. "May I take this?"

"Please, don't let me interfere. Go for it."

I answered on the fourth ring. "Hi."

"How is it going?"

"Pretty well."

"Find someone yet?"

"Maybe."

"Well, call me when you do. I want to meet the paragon who will be protecting my wife."

"Will do."

Click.

"I'm sorry about the interruption, where were we?"

"My not-exactly-you primary objective."

I bit my lip, trying to figure out a way to phrase my situation. "My husband and I have a...a...an unusual relationship. I want out, but I don't think he'll let me go."

"You need a good divorce lawyer, not a bodyguard."

"You don't understand." I pulled down the neckline on my turtleneck top and revealed the faded green finger marks. "This is because I wanted to go to the mall by myself. He has eyes constantly on me, and I asked him if I could get a female bodyguard so I could go shopping without him sending his hired guns along."

"I see."

Did she? "I want to learn self-defense. I want to start a new life, and I want to disappear off the radar. My husband is wealthy and powerful. He has the resources to do as he pleases. If I can fade away for 7 years, I'll be declared legally dead. I'll be free."

"I could help you. But it will cost more than a salary. Your husband is Jakob Haytham, correct?"

"Yes."

"CEO and COO of Haytham Science Labs?"

"Yes, the one and the same."

"Since we're being unflinchingly honest with one another, how much do you know of your husband's work?"

"Not much, he doesn't discuss it with me. I do know he started a new project, but I have no idea what it is about."

Zamara grabbed her briefcase and after laying it on her lap, opened it. She pulled out a manila folder and put it on the small table. "Your husband had three contracts with the United States Government. Two have been fulfilled. The third keeps being put off. Surveillance of the lab shows traces of radioactive elements. Geiger counters sing like an opera soprano within half a mile of his lab. That's not a good sign." She opened the folder and pulled out an eight by ten photo, then slid it over to me. "Do you recognize this man?"

Shocked, I replied, "Yes, that's Morgan Stratham, my husband's bodyguard."

"He's also a drug courier."

I was startled and unnerved that the interview I had now turned into a mild interrogation - and not by me. "Why do you have a file on my husband's activities? How do you know about his contracts and think Morgan is a courier?"

"Mrs. Haytham, while I may no longer work for the FBI in the same capacity as I once did, the agency has had an eye on your husband and his work for *quite* some time. Your husband is a very famous man, you know. How are your wrists doing?"

"What do you mean?"

"Surveillance when you were in Nice honeymooning showed you had bruises on your wrists."

"You spied on us when we were in France?"

"Not so much on you. More of when your husband when wasn't around you."

"Why does the FBI have such an interest in my husband? What did he do?"

"He's done a few things. He's engineering bio war-machines. That's a big no-no. He also has sexual tastes not many entertain, and unfortunately some of his partners have come up missing."

"What? Even the government knows he likes BDSM?" Has she judged me because I married him? Guilty by association? While there are certain aspects of sex with Christos I didn't enjoy in the least, some things he did were kinky-fun that I did like.

With a cold look in her eye, Zamara Malone spoke in a low tone. "Madam, your husband may call it BDSM, but it is not, not in the way defined as Safe, Sane and Consensual. Google what real BDSM is, get educated. Don't buy into everything your husband tells you."

I wanted to hug Zamara, knowing that I wasn't wrong in how I felt about my husband.

"Why does the government care about my husband's sexual tastes?"

"The government doesn't, not like I do. You see, my twin sister, Aisha, was one of his subs. I want to find her, or what's left of her. Only your husband has the answer. You looking for a female bodyguard is great luck on my part. You help me find my sister and I'll keep your bully at bay."

Chapter Three

After Zamara's revelation, I was floored.

That briefcase Christos said was protection from subs trying to blackmail him? All those photos of his subs? According to the FBI expert, serial killers often take photos of their victims, so they can relive the moment, sometimes keep trinkets, like jewelry. Pretty horrific stuff. But do I believe this woman over my husband?

As intense Christos could get, I didn't think him capable of making me disappear- I mean, he has the resources to make it happen, but I'm his wife, not a sub. That's a huge difference.

"Is it?" I asked myself. "He has final say in all matters... How is that much different than a sub? To him, Wife means Full Time Sub. When I married him, signing the marriage license was like signing a contract binding me to his whims for life."

True, Christos had a penchant for embracing the same old thing when it comes to women he spoils, but that doesn't mean I'm going to end up missing, not like those poor lost souls who surrendered to him. I fought. I didn't want to be a sub. *They did, and weren't offered a wedding ring.*

They stayed with him until they mysteriously disappeared.

It's so much to take in. Aisha and other missing subs, Christos being under government surveillance, Morgan being a drug mule, and the bio war-machines. Zamara let me read everything in the manila folder. Most of it related to Christos' laboratory and his work there, dealing with radioactivity and the bio war-machines. When Zamara explained what they were, my jaw dropped. Shit is straight out of a horror movie that possessed an unlimited budget and no moral sense of responsibility.

Bio war-machines were people tainted with a virus/bacteria hybrid referenced as Project ELJ3763, Virteria Serum, bound together in a biofilm. An injection with the serum would make each person into an exponential killing machine. They could be airdropped into a location to assault. Once the biofilm dissolves, the Virteria are unleashed into the bloodstream. It attacks nerve centers, causing the infected to feel no pain. It also goes for the brain, to certain neurotransmitters, which would cause one to hunger for blood. Their saliva would infect the bitten, and so forth it would go, to infect all the populace.

Zombie-vampires for the win. According to Zamara, Christos designed the Virteria to have a secondary effect. If a tainted person bit another already infected, they acted as a "salted bomb," exploding and the "debris" left over, incredibly radioactive- enough that a pinky-sized piece of tainted flesh would contaminate a square mile. Once the infected person's skin began to crystalize, skin cells look like glitter and refract the light. That's basically when the "bomb is armed." Now imagine people getting bit, spreading out, contaminating all until nothing is left but the twinkling tainted biting each other.

Ka.

Boom.

I couldn't believe it, seemed so far-fetched.

Zamara and I stayed in the hotel room for a few hours- I cancelled all the other interviews and thanked them for their time before digging into the file.

After the bio war-machines were explained to me, Zamara and I discussed her fraternal twin, Aisha- she subbed before Belinda, Christos' official last sub. And then, before we parted, Zamara laid out a plan for my escape, the entire time I took mental notes.

"When we go shopping, if you can, start taking out cash when you make a purchase. It's harder to trace than ATM transactions. I can hide it for you. You could sell your jewelry, but it could be traced. Best bet is to get cash now and keep it out of his reach. I'll get you a cell, that way you have a helpline if he takes your Blackberry away- you won't want to take that with you, as the GPS on it can be tracked. If you want to disappear, I know the perfect place to hide you. Do you like to read much, Mrs. Haytham?"

"Yes, love to read. And please, call me Selli."

"Then get your hands on a copy of *My Side of the Mountain*, Selli. It'll be relevant."

In a state of trepidation and anxiety, I drove home from the motel, wondering if everything that happened this afternoon would be visible on my face. Could he tell I found an ally who'd help me escape? Had to remind myself to breathe. Act like everything is fine. Act like I'm happy I found someone who'd take me shopping to my heart's content. Act like I'm tired, having conducted interviews all damned day. *Just act normal.*

When I walked into the living room, Christos sat in a wing-backed chair, legs crossed. He turned and faced me as I entered the room. "So, how did it go?"

"Found my bodyguard. She's got great fashion sense, too."

"Really. That's nice. When do I meet her?"

"Tomorrow morning, bright and early."

"What's she like?"

"She's business-like. Not much for idle chatter."

"Well, can't wait to meet her. If she's going to protect that which I consider mine safe, then she and I will have a little talk."

"You don't need to have a little talk with her, Christos. She knows what she's doing."

Oh crap. His nose flared. That's like the starting flag of his mood swing. "You were gone a long time today, Selesta."

"I had a lot of interviews."

"Yes. I also know you didn't you the small conference room like we agreed."

Like he agreed. "Figured I'd conduct the interviews in private, like when I first asked about getting the bodyguard."

"Next time, tell me."

"Yes, Christos."

He stood up and walked over to me. "You didn't sound sincere, Selli. I was very upset to discover you weren't where I thought you were supposed to be. Do not do it again."

"Yes, Christos. I won't do it again."

A small smile emerged from his lips. "That's my beautiful, brave girl."

I tried to smile back. "I think I'm going to take a bath. Are we dining in, tonight?"

"Yes, you are. I have to head back to the laboratory and finish up the spectrum analysis. This project is too special to be trusted in just anyone's hands."

"What is your project? You never have told me what genius you're cooking up in your lab."

A broad smile split Christos' face. "My wife, you will be a queen, when the project is done. That's all you need to know. You will be a queen, and you will bear the fruit of a new world, my beautiful, beautiful, girl. It'll be just you, me, and ours."

Chapter Four

I think I pushed the line when I didn't adhere to Christos' demand of using the hotel's conference room. The way his manner changed when he said he knew I wasn't there, I thought something bad was going to happen. I wanted to vacate the room and find a little nook to hide in until his rage calmed down.

Whenever I cross that damned arbitrary line, he grudgefucks me. I'm tired of it. Too rough and more often than not, I come out with bruises. It's one thing to be tied up using something with a little give, it's another when the rope or handcuffs bite into me hard enough to leave colorful marks that last for days. Or when he deliberately marks me so I can't go to the beach any more. Sigh.

I took a long bath while Christos went about his business at the lab. Didn't know how long he'd be gone, but I'd enjoy every moment in blissful solitude. The roman tub became my refuge from the emotional roller coaster Christos arranged for me to ride. As bubbles floated and popped around me, I lost myself in thought, pondering all the ways he uses to make me capitulate.

He yells. Stalks off and comes back, still angry. He's grabbed me with unnecessary force. He's cajoled and he's left me to stew and wonder if he'd ever be back. He's never really protected me, despite all the security detail and Morgan Stratham. He can't protect me from his rages or tendency to go too far.

Still can't believe Morgan's been hauling the Virteria serum from Christos' lab to some place in the California Bay Area. The depth of the depravity ate at me, to think I trusted so blindly in someone who could betray mankind like that. But should I be so surprised considering the passions Christos entertains?

Didn't know what to do other than get away. Even if the Virteria serum is a hoax, I knew I couldn't survive living with Christos and his unpredictability. One can walk on eggshells only so long before one cracks. I can't believe I married the first man I screwed, a man who helped me get drunk more times than I count so he could do whatever he liked with my intoxicated body. That's rape. If I wouldn't agree when sober, to get me foxed to the point where it actually sounded like a good idea *is rape*. It's hard to wrap one's mind around that notion, that first love isn't necessarily the longest lasting, nor the person one gives heart and soul to, being worth the heartache.

Can't say how long I lingered in that tub. Water went cool and bubbles evaporated by the time I pulled the plug. Got out, dried off. Spied myself in the wall-length mirror while wrapping the fuzzy black robe around my body. Bruises faded away and I could look at myself without cringing, as I hate seeing myself marked, especially when I hadn't agreed on being bruised beforehand.

When I turned around to enter the bedroom, I saw Christos laying on the bed, shirtless, with his khaki pants hanging low on his hips.

"Home already?"

Christos rolled over and looked at me. "Yes. Got halfway there before I changed my mind. The analysis can wait until tomorrow."

I didn't like this—it's unlike Christos to change his mind so abruptly about his work. My sense of foreboding grew as my husband continued talking. "I decided we needed to talk." He stood up and walked my way.

Silently, I stood in the door's threshold, anxiously awaiting Christos' discussion. He'd have his say and I'd go along, that way I don't provoke him to anger. Nod and smile when the American Psycho talks.

"Inform your new security detail that we're flying into SFO in three days. We'll be there less than a week."

SFO? "Where is SFO?"

"San Fran. Ever see the Golden Gate Bridge?"

"No, can't say I have. Why are we going there?"

"Going to open a secondary laboratory in Berkeley. There's a ribbon cutting thing to attend. Got a grant from UC Berkeley, and have recruited some of their brightest minds."

"You never told me you were going to open another lab! Going to cure cancer?" Or cause a cancer on society?

Christos smiled down at me, apparently pleased with my ego stroking. "I wish I had that technology. No, this is for the military."

My heart thundered in my ears. Could it be that Zamara was telling the truth? This is probably as close to a confession as I'd get from him. I changed the topic. "Darling, can I ask a question?"

"You just did. But yes, you can ask another."

"Why can't I call you Chris?"

I could have sworn lightening flew from his eyes. "Because I prefer you not to do so. Jakob Christos. I'm more Christ-like than you, and I won't let anyone forget or lessen that. I have beauty, youth and wealthy. I'm the new Christ, born to save the world. My childhood prepared me for the cruelty of humanity. I was forged in the fires of hell. The strength given to me will help save the world, wait and see, my beautiful girl."

Tried not to gasp at the megalomaniac standing before me. "Truly?" He went to an English boarding school as a kid, silver spoon in hand. His family has connections—his uncle is a senator. Christos' mother was a socialite and his father, worked for a laboratory run by DuPont.

"The night you gave me *carte blanche* in punishing you with a broom handle you proved yourself worthy. The pain you endured was but a lick of Hades' Flames. You bend to my will, time and again, like you would your king. You have shown yourself a worthy mate to me. Because of your loyalty, you will be rewarded, for you and only you are worthy to bear my seed."

I didn't give him permission to hit me with a broom handle. I told him I didn't want to have sex. He didn't hear, and didn't like when I fought back. That was only a couple weeks after the wedding. Two years later and he's still bringing it back up, only painted in a perverse light of unwilling consent.

The more Christos spoke, the more I realized he took a train to NutsoLand and missed the last exit, and was heading straight into the WTF Sea. So far, everything he's said has corroborated what Zamara told me.

"Come, wife. You need to reward me for letting you get a new bodyguard. You owe me for that which I have given you. And I've given you quite a lot, now haven't I?"

I swallowed. But this is what I agreed to, whether or not I realized it when I walked down the aisle to have and to hold Christos. Stewed at the notion that I had to pay back my husband for something he completely takes for granted, at the point of ignoring what Morgan says. What good is a bodyguard when one doesn't let them guard one's body?

Sigh. I knew this would be a long night that would end in extensive bruising. I can handle it, for a while at least. Long enough to pretend I'm happy and nothing will change that. But as soon as I can, I'm getting the hell out. I didn't agree to marry Christ^2. God knows, this could end with me crucified, literally or figuratively.

Fuck that shit.

Chapter Five

I tried to hide my excitement of seeing San Francisco for the first time. It was, as assured by pop culture, foggy, busy, and filled with counter-culture rebels. I experienced the foggy and busy part. Missed out on the counter-culture since Christos avoids that scene like the plague. And yes, I'm mildly disappointed with that, as I would have loved to experience Haight-Ashbury for myself. Alas.

So, I didn't do the tourist-y thing I anticipated, not until the third day. The first two days were spent in my luxury suite, recuperating from me "rewarding" Christos for being so generous as to get me a bodyguard of my own gender, while he spent most of his time at the new lab. Such a sweetie pie, with his conditional benevolence. The torment he chose this time left bruises on my throat, wrists and ankles. He tied me with rough hempen rope to the bed posts, face down. Christos chose a dog choke chain as my collar. He'd stimulate me with an intense vibrator then pull on the choke chain, tightening it as the tension built in my nethers. He'd loosen the collar when I started to black out. Over and over, all night long.

I hated it.

The chain left a pattern of marks on my throat. Glad I bought the turtlenecks when I did, because I needed them badly. I didn't see Zamara until the third day. When she came in, she held a finger to her lips in warning of silence. From her pocket, she pulled out a black contraption, extended it to almost twice its length. She pushed a button and a display of lights flashed, then settled on green. Zamara swept it around the room, not missing a square inch. When she swept by the phone and by the bed, the lights blinked and remained red. She knelt down by the bed, and peeked beneath. Zamara's head popped back up, and she gestured for me to come by her. When I reached her side, she pointed to her eyes, and then pointed to a place under the bed. I took that as meaning I should see what she spotted. As she moved out of the way, Zamara collapsed her little detector and put it in her pocket.

Digital recorder, taped to the headboard, under the box spring. An idea came. "Zamara, let's go shopping." Anger poured through me. Being spied on by one's husband has that tendency, I guess.

"Yes, Mrs. Haytham. I will have the car out front in two minutes." She left the room, and I followed, picking my purse up as we exited the posh prison.

Zamara went to the parking garage and hopped into a car I never seen before. It looked slick and definitely not American. I didn't recognize the emblem, either. As soon as I shut the car door and buckled up, she said, "Your husband told me I wasn't needed for a couple days. So I drove down. Are you okay?"

"Yes. Just tired and bruised."

"Bruises heal. As long as you have your spirit, you'll survive."

"Yay."

"Where to, boss?"

"Have you ever been here before?"

Zamara nodded.

"Then you know more than I do. Although I want to hit Lush. Is there a Lush store here?"

"Yep." And away we went, migrating through a hodgepodge of one-way streets and never-ending hills. When I spotted my first trolley, the jingle for Rice-a-Roni went through my head. Couldn't help it. The brisk salt air, the freedom from my suite and husband, oh, it was a great feeling. Wasn't long before Zamara spoke again. "We're being followed."

My heart raced like a hundred greyhounds after a fat rabbit. "Do you know who they are?"

"They are puds with no idea how to remain undetected. Look behind us, the two guys in the little blue Miata. They followed us out of the parking garage. Either they want to hit Lush too, or they are tailing us."

"Can we escape them?"

"Yes, but not today. We don't want your husband to think you can easily disappear; otherwise he might tighten the watch. When you get back to your room, call family or a friend. Say something specific. And then see if your husband uses what you say in conversation. Bet you he will."

I sat in silence until we reached a parking structure somewhere down town. Hated the idea that Christos would spy on me. It was bad enough when I was working, I mean, he bought the damn company I worked for just so he could keep tabs on me. Had no idea where we were, other than it being a busy shopping district. Didn't take long for me to do some retail therapy. Zamara guided me on what sort of things I should get for my escape. Some heavy clothes, which seemed appropriate and could be passed off as needed for the early spring weather striking San Fran. Hiking boots. I bought an e-reader for entertainment, although the tactile sensation of paper betwixt fingers cannot be replaced by technology. While at Lush, I bought henna for my hair and other scentual bliss creature comforts. Zamara said I would need them for where I was going.

My Side of the Mountain. Never heard of that book, but with my new e-reader, I delved into the young adult story of a boy fleeing to the mountains, living in the wild, and whose main contact with the outside world is a librarian.

Aside from languorous time in the bathtub, some bouts of vanilla sex with Christos and random shopping trips with Zamara hoarding my supplies out of my husband's reach, my time in California bored me. I was forbidden from venturing into the risqué parts of the city under threat of the choke chain. I did as Zamara suggested, and called my mother. I told her about being in San Francisco and she had her moment of *squeee*. Then she asked how Christos and I were doing.

"We're okay."

"Just okay? That man you chose seems kind of intense. You sure you're okay?"

"I'm fine, really. Picked you up some Happy Hippy from Lush." Needed to change the topic so I wouldn't start bawling.

I didn't sign up for full-time bondage. Best I recall, I put my foot down because that flavor of passion isn't exactly my cup of tea. He never really respected it. Sure, he turned things down a notch, but when pissed, he lashes out, by paddle, belt, or hand.

I asked myself, "If your life was happening to a friend, and she felt the way you do, what would you tell her?"

"Run. Fast. Don't stop."

The day before we were scheduled to fly out, Christos got all romantic and took me to the wharf. We meandered through all the piers, and walked up a hill to the Magical Land of Chocolate, also known as Ghirardelli Square. Up a series of steps, and before us stood a bronze water fountain in the shape of a mermaid sitting on a rock. I stared, mesmerized by the detail and patina of the art before me. After a moment, I turned away. Christos led me on to the gift store and we stocked up on chocolate.

Laden with bags, my husband ended up hailing a horse drawn carriage driver.

"The Mandarin Oriental Hotel," Christos said as we entered the conveyance.

The man in Victorianesque clothes nodded his head, clamped his top hat on a bit tighter and flicked the rains. The black horses trotted off, and we wove through throngs of people. I could see the bay, and Alcatraz situated like a ship in the bay. Christos leaned in and whispered. "I'll give you the world, my beautiful girl. But if you ever betray me, I know exactly where I'll hide your body."

Chapter Six

I know exactly where I'll hide your body.

While I resented the dark recesses of Christos' passion, informing me that he's given some thought as how he'd make me disappear should I displease him, seriously upped the ante for me. This is like a whole new boss level of a video game. One life, no restarts, fairies, or potions, what I have is what I got.

Not comforting.

Anxiety hit hard, I tried not shaking like a leaf anytime I looked at my beloved husband. He's thought about killing me. That scares the shit out of me like none other.

We arrived at the Mandarin Oriental and made our way to the suite. I wanted a bubble bath to soak away the tension, but I didn't want to draw one when Christos was there. I didn't want to be drowned in a tub of Lush bubbles.

Instead, I lay on the bed, mindful of the little recorder below my head. "Christos, I want to thank you for letting me have a female body guard. I've enjoyed my retail therapy."

"See, that's what I've been telling you. Go shopping; you can afford whatever your heart desires now. Glad to see you finally doing as I said." *Glad I obeyed him like a good wife should.*

My heart wants freedom, could he afford that? "It was awkward to go with Morgan. He never said anything of the sort, but I bet he hates shopping." I'm not fond of shopping myself, especially spending someone else's money. But the sprees here in San Fran, were as I reasoned Christos' payment for emotional damages. I'm sparing him the fun of being in a court of law and helping myself to half of his fortune instead, since he's so concerned about the paparazzi.

"Morgan is not paid to have an opinion on the subject." Christos said it so drolly, I wasn't sure if he was joking or not.

"Whether he's paid for his opinions or not, he's still entitled to them."

"Not when he's on the clock."

Does no good to argue. "What time are we flying out tomorrow?" I did and I did not want to go back home.

"I'm staying. You'll fly out in the morning."

"By myself? Zamara drove down. Am I taking Morgan, instead?" Wonder why he's staying, something with the lab… But what? Christos has seemed almost preoccupied lately. A part of me wants to blame it on the new lab. The other part wants to blame it on the things happening in the lab.

"Your security detail drove from Redmond to San Francisco? I'm not reimbursing her for gasoline."

"I don't think that's an issue, Christos. But yes, she drove."

"Then you'll either drive back with her or she'll fly with you."

"I'll drive back with her. Promise, we won't go Thelma and Louise." Although, the thought does have potential now that I know I'm disposable to him. "It'll be an adventure, going up 101 and traversing through parts unknown."

Christos cracked a smile. "I'll expect you waiting in bed for me. Naked."

Smiled as best I could. "Yes, sir."

"That's more like it." The wee smile grew into a grin. "When you get all submissive, it's nice. Nice for you not to argue for once."

"Having an opinion isn't the same as arguing."

"Says you."

"Yep, says me. So how much longer will you be down here before you head home?"

"Perhaps a couple days, maybe another week. Depends on whether the stable isotopes can be controlled."

"Damn those rogue isotopes."

"That's what I've been saying in more colorful language."

My mind tread in dark places. I couldn't help it. "Christos, can I ask you something?"

"Yes."

"Why did you say what you said in the carriage?"

He looked at me with his raptor eyes, ever seeing, ever knowing. "What did I say in the carriage?"

Seriously? "You said if I ever betrayed you, you know where you'd hide my body. I want to know why you would say something like that."

"I don't know what you're talking about. You feeling okay?" His words were concerned, but his tone was not. The timbre of his voice edged toward predator. Christos' face, an emotionless mask of superiority.

"No games, Christos, please. Just level with me."

"I said it in the heat of the moment. I've got a lot riding on this project. A lot. It fails, we're fucked. Not just you and me, but a lot more people."

"Will you tell me about your laboratory endeavor?"

"Can't. It's classified."

I frowned. "How fucked are we talking about?"

"Wish I could tell you."

"So I'm heading home and eagerly anticipating your arrival, whenever it may be?"

"Yes. But before you go, I want you to go shopping. Go to here," Christos walked over and handed me a business card. Off-white matte paper had the words LOLI'S FUNLAND and an address. "Pick something out."

"Okay… what am I looking for?" Loli's Funland sounded almost ominous.

"Whatever your heart desires. It's a sex shop. I want you to pick something out for us to play with when I get home. Anything you want."

"Anything?"

"Within reason."

"Strap-on, so I can peg you?"

Christos did a double take. "You want to explore pegging?"

"Just trying to find your hard limit." *And/or shock you.*

"I'm not keen on the idea of pegging. Although… If you wanted to get DP'd, I'd be up for that."

"What's *DP'd?*"

"It means double penetration."

"Oh." Yeah, no thanks. Not with him.

"Get some lingerie, too. I have an idea."

"You want to wear lingerie with me?"

"No." He shot me a disgusted look that I rather enjoyed. "I want to take your picture."

"Thought you said you'd never take my picture, like you did your subs."

"This is different. I'm thinking more calendar girl."

"I'm not really keen on that idea, Christos. Calendar girl or bondage girl, I'd rather there be no photos."

"You wouldn't do that for me?"

"I'm just not comfortable with the idea." Especially knowing serial killers do that sort of thing.

Christos stood next to the bed. He grabbed me by the arm and hauled me into a sitting position. "Look, Selli. There are few things I want of you, your compliance being one of them. Listen well, my wife." He held my chin so I had no option but to look into his darkening eyes. "Next time your security detail waves her little magic wand around in my living space, will be the last time she works. I will ruin her."

My heart beat fast. How did he know?

"Also, you shouldn't mind me taking photos of you, considering you are on camera almost 24/7."

"What?"

"There are eight security cameras hidden in this suite. There are well over a hundred in our home. You are always on camera, Selli. Always. Get used to it."

"That's a huge invasion of privacy, Christos."

"No it's not. You're my wife, you have no privacy. On your little car trip with your security detail, you best iterate that I'm the one who pays her, and that her career is at stake. Enjoy that ride, because when you get home, you'll start changing your mind about certain topics. I don't think you want to be trained. That choke chain can work wonders."

I need to go shopping again. Need to get away from him before he gets back home. I need away from him before the Hell and high water come flooding my way.

Chapter Seven

Oh my god. Shit hit the fan.

In a flurry of worry, I packed my bags and had them ready, by the door, for when Zamara came the next morning. I didn't let her carry any of the bags out, I did it all, as a way to burn off my anger. Christos was in Berkeley, doing his mad scientist thing. No doubt he'd watch the security feed and get all gleeful about how wound up I am.

When Zamara and I went shopping before we headed north out of San Fran, she and I went over the plan for escape. The opportunity Christos gave by not traveling with me home was just the opportunity I needed to grasp my freedom with both hands.

"He wanted me to tell you, that should you get nosey in his living space by 'waving your magic wand,' he'll ruin you." I felt dirty, relaying Christos' words to Zamara.

"I've made quite the impression then? Good. Means his focus is off you, somewhat. Here," she put a tiny box in my hand as we sat in her Melling Wildcat roadster, waiting for traffic to cooperate. A marathon through the city did not help. "This is your lifeline. Carry it with you at all times. Put it in your bra or something. I've programmed a couple numbers in it. The one marked 'Tyb' is our contact. He's great at hiding things."

"What kind of things?"

"Anything. Here, hand me the phone." I did as she asked. She flipped the phone open and dialed the pre-programmed number. She held a finger up as she spoke, smiling wide the whole time. "Hey, Tyb, it's Mara… Got a new project for you. Are you in?… Good. Need you to make someone disappear… No, alive, needs to stay that way. … Not a hostage sitch. Almost a Patty Hearst, but no banks and guns and she's willing… She'll tell you her story if you ask nice. Just don't be a prick, okay? She's a lady… No, Tyb, not British aristocracy." Zamara sighed. "Fine. Operation Swan Dive. … Subject's code name is Egon. I'm Janine and you are Slimer. Happy now? We'll be in your neck of the woods in about five hours, maybe longer because of traffic. I'll call you again on this number when we're at an hour's ETA to arrange rendezvous point Alpha." Zamara folded the phone shut and handed it back to me. "Why are brothers such ass monkeys?"

"Tyb is your brother?" My mind whirled with the one-sided conversation I heard. This was going to be interesting.

"Yeah. The only sane one out of the three of us. He's perfect for your escape. Tyb lives way up in the hills on a little self-sufficient homestead. He's totally off the grid. He doesn't even have a government-issued identification card. As far as most people are concerned, he doesn't exist. He died in a teenage car wreck. Did you read that book, by the way?"

"*My Side of the Mountain*? Yes, finished it."

"Tyb's like that. Wait until you see his house. The way it's designed, set into the hillside, it's almost undetectable by air. If you don't know the way, you won't find it."

"And I'm going to stay with him until I'm declared legally dead?"

"Possibly. Depends on how things roll. May have to move you out of the country, we'll play it by ear. My suggestion to you is to get some stationary while we're out, write letters to friends and family and let them know what's going on. Tell them that Christos will lie to save face. If he gets wind that you're still around, then he will badger them. Tell them not to believe him, and that you will periodically contact them so they know you're okay. You have to warn them about Christos, because he'll try to use his money and influence to cajole information. I'll mail the letters for you. Christos won't be able to intercept them once they are in the mail system. Just don't email them. The IP number can be traced to a general location, unless it's through a proxy service, but even that's not fool-proof. Especially when it's Jakob Haytham getting thwarted. Did you hear what he did to the Chinese factory who made incorrect parts for his laboratory's containment block?"

I shook my head in the negative. Had no clue. Couldn't have been good.

"Via video feed, he ordered the supervisors to beat the laborers with bamboo canes, one by one in front of the camera.

Then he had the manager beat the supervisors. Then your husband ordered the manager to kill himself. When the dumbfounded manager just sat there, one of the government officials who arranged the video feed shot the manager in the head. When a man with wealth and no morals wants something done, there is no price he won't pay."

A knot formed in my throat and I tried wrapping my mind around the thought of just how ruthless Christos was under his demeanor of socially awkward, repressed, and tortured scientist. What would he do to me if he discovered I planned to disappear?

My pulse thundered in my ears. So soon! "How am I going to get away from him?"

"You're going to die. Nighttime on a dark and winding road… Car crash over a cliff and into the ocean. We're going to cut and bleach your hair. Your clothes with be found, some of your hair. Your belongings. But your body, gone, assumed to have fed sharks, crabs, and hagfish. If Christos has any life insurance out on you, well, we'll just see how long it takes for him to cash in on it. He might try pulling strings to have you declared legally dead before seven years."

We drove over the Golden Gate Bridge and through a tunnel. Then through trees. We pulled off into a small city and I asked to hit a SuperCuts to get my hair done. "No. We stop there, you'd be on camera from the parking lot, on. We don't want Christos to find out you cut your hair short, and if there you are, on security camera, getting shorn like a sheep… defeats the idea of hiding your appearance from him."

"Got it." I hope Zamara is as talented with cutting hair as she is knowledgeable about camera feeds. How much longer until we contact Tyb?"

"Eh, about two hours. We need to get closer to Willits. He's up the hill in Laytonville."

"Is there anything I should know about him?" Curiosity niggled at my mind as to what this brother of Zamara's would be like.

"Yeah. Don't tell Tyb who your husband is until he warms up to you. Otherwise you might be staying in the treehouse and left to fight the squirrels for their nuts."

Chapter Eight

Two squiggling lines of black rubber marred the road, snaking towards the ocean twinkling with silvered moonlight. Below the steep cliff side, a pile of ancient rocks cradled a sports car, engulfed in flames. The heat rising from the wreckage toasted my cheeks.

Behind me, winds beat furiously against mighty redwoods surrounding the turnout, as the helicopter lifting Zamara's Wildcat away from the scene made its escape. A cloud of curly black hair whipped around Zamara's face as she asked loudly, "Where are you putting my ride?"

A deep male voice answered with a mocking tone, "In storage. But I got you a *sweet* Honda Accord. You don't mind a little four-banger, do you?"

"You're an asshole, Tyb. My Melling is a V10, and you're sticking me with a V4. Evil."

"Just a little, I think I get it from you. It's the Accord or the Mule, but I have a hard time picturing you in a 4-wheel golf cart, and I don't want to haul goat feed in the Accord."

"You're doing this because you're still pissed off about the El Camino? Tell me that has nothing to do with sticking me with a shitty little four-banger."

"That may or may not have something to do with it. But seriously, I'm down on spare cars for you to total. Sorry."

I stood between the two, with the bags of stuff I wasn't willing to sacrifice sitting at my feet. A delicate cough and their attention focused on lil ol' me. "So what do we do now? Wait here for the popos?"

Zamara spoke. "I have some things to accomplish. I'll be up at the homestead in about a week. Watch the news, and keep an ear to the ground. If you need anything let me know, Tyb. I'll bring it up when I make my way back."

"Alrighty, little sis. Don't get blown up."

"There's not enough ANFO or C4 to keep me down. Don't get arrested, boy-o."

I piped up. "Virteria serum?"

"Well, that *might* slow me down a bit. Take care of her, Tyb. She's important. And if she likes you, she might even tell you her real name." With that, Zamara whirled around and trotted down the road to the awaiting car.

Tyb bent and picked up the bags at my feet and began walking across the road and trekking up the hill. I scrambled behind, not wanting to get lost in the dark. We walked in silence for about five minutes before coming across a parked vehicle on a dirt road. Looked like an older muscle car. He popped open the door, chucked my stuff in the back seat and hopped in the driver's seat. I got in, buckled up. "Do you and Zamara do this often? Hide people?"

"More often than I'd care to admit. She usually has a really good reason for wanting someone to disappear. What's your reason for pulling a Houdini?"

"My husband wants to take over the world and have me be the mother of a new breed of man." That was said with no irony. "He's batshit crazy and I needed to get away before he gets even more psychotic."

"Get a divorce lawyer and restraining order."

I laughed. "That's pretty much what your sister said. Wish it were that simple."

"Everything is that simple when you put it in the right context."

"I have yet to master that trick."

"You and me both. So, what am I supposed to call you?"

"Izzy for now."

"Izzy? Can do. So, Izzy, you have some farm experience?"

"You can hope in one hand and sneeze in the other. See which gets filled first."

"A cynic? This will be entertaining. So no farm experience. Been around animals?"

"Just the bipedal kind."

"No animal experience. Greenthumb, maybe?"

"I wish. I have a black thumb of death." Every houseplant I ever had, has met an untimely demise. Don't know how, I mean I watered and fertilized them. Sunlight, too. But plants just don't like me. It's a fact.

A moment of silence, then Tyb's velvety voice returned. "So, what did you do to occupy your time?"

"Was a bookseller. Then housewife in a gilded cage."

"So I get to school you? Oh, the joy. Please tell me you are a fast learner." Sarcasm must be a family trait.

"I am. If I can see it done and understand the logic behind it, memorizing tasks isn't an issue."

"Good to know."

"Zamara told me you live on a homestead? Sounds pioneerish." That, and asking about my expertise at manual labor, foretold the level of *interesting* I could be sure to enjoy.

"Yeah. Built it myself. I raise my own stock, grow my own food. Make my own biodiesel and beer."

"How can you do all that, and stay off the radar?"

"Easy. My dad owns the land and its fenced off to keep hunters and hikers away. I grow a good portion of my edibles in a food forest. Bunch of berries, grapes, nuts, pears, apples, even have Satsuma Mandarins. I use a meadow to grow grain for bread and animal feed. You'll just have to see it. Can you shoot?"

"Shoot what, hoops?"

"Gun, bow, crossbow...?"

"Nope. Just hoops."

"Are you afraid of guns?"

"No. Just afraid of the devastation they can bring."

"Good answer. Tomorrow, I'll teach you to shoot a revolver. Long guns are more accurate, but in close quarters, a pistol will do. I want you to carry it with you at all times."

"Why?"

"I live in the woods. Animals with pointy teeth and/or big claws show up every now and again. I don't want you helpless if you're out feeding the goats or plucking cackleberries. The dogs can do so much, but I want to be on the safe side. If anything is up or you need help, you can fire a round as a signal."

"Dogs?" I had images of bulldogs and Labradors.

"Maremmas. Livestock guardian dogs. I have a pack that oversees the goats and cow. Do you like cheese?"

"Love it." That was the best part of my honeymoon, the reveling in a plethora of French cheeses.

"Good. After shooting, I'll teach you to milk dairy critters, then make cheese and butter. You're on egg detail, too. Are you afraid of chickens?"

"Don't know, never been around them before." Never imagined myself plucking *cackleberries*.

In the dark, Tyb turned his head and smiled my way for a brief moment. "Well, Izzy darling, I'm going to drop a lot of knowledge on you tomorrow. Hope it won't hurt." With expertise, he drove on winding dirt roads in the dark. Then the sound of static startled me. After a split second, a woman's voice spoke in a jargon I didn't understand.

Tyb spoke in the brief lull between communications on the radio. "Police scanner. Someone reported an accident south of Elk. Gee, wonder what that could be."

I listened in shock and horrific excitement at the emergency services converse back and forth about the situation. I felt horrible that those emergency workers were wasting their time searching for someone who wasn't there. I felt horrible about the worry and cost that my disappearance would cost everyone but Jakob Christos Haytham.

"How did you arrange for a helicopter to pick up your sister's car?" Because that's something an average Joe wouldn't or couldn't do.

"I collect favors from people like some collect stamps. I just called in a favor from a friend with access to a helicopter."

In silence I sat, as Tyb navigated his way home. The constant turns of the mountain road made me feel ill, so I cracked a window. Instantly, the car smelled like a skunk. "Holy crap! Does it always reek up here?"

"I take it you aren't familiar with this area. Izzy, you are in the Emerald Triangle. That stink is the smell of money growing on the mountainside."

I didn't follow what he was saying. "What now?"

"Cannabis. Lots and lots of *mari-ju-wanna*." The way Tyb said it brought a smile to my face.

"Pot, huh? You're right, I'm clueless about this area."

"Mendocino, Trinity and Humboldt counties are notorious for their pot culture. They make up the Emerald Triangle."

"I see." I didn't know what else to say. "So… how much longer until we get to your place?"

"About three hours."

Shit. I leaned my head toward to cracked window, letting the skunky air pelt my face in an attempt to not heave chunks everywhere. I hate getting car sick.

Tyb's voice entered my ear. "Get some rest, I'll wake you up when we get to the hiking point."

Hikinkg point? "What's that?"

"We have to hike three miles to the house. Think one stays hidden by having a road right to their front door?"

I am a city girl despite my small town roots. Hiking, farming, fetching eggs and groping dairy animals seemed as foreign as alien life. But lurking behind the overwhelming notion of homesteading was the threat of Christos finding me. Nothing scares me more than my husband finding me. For certain, the choke chain would be the least of my worries.

Cackleberries.

Yeah. I can do this.

PART TWO
HER FREEDOM

Chapter Nine

I was in a warm, comfortable place that smelled a lot like my stoner aunt's house; that is to say *earthy* in a patchouli kind of way. Somewhere, I hovered between the world of sleep devoid of dreams and land of the awake. My eyes closed, I heard a man's voice say, "Lady Dunklebee, 'skit 'er up."

For a moment, I forgot where I was and who owned that voice. Oh yeah. Tyb's place. After tingles of anxiety slowly evaporated, I noticed a small dog of regal bearing walking sedately into my room, head and tail carried high. It stopped by the bed and began to howl loud enough to blister ears.

I sat up. "Okay, okay! I'm awake." That was enough to stop the mutt from caterwauling. It turned around and trotted out, its nails making click-click sounds on the hardwood floor. I thrust my arms in the air and stretched. My legs hurt from last night's hike. Not paying attention to Tyb meant I walked right into a mine field of thorny blackberries. Skin and clothes all got snagged on the spikes, a lesson not forgotten. Blackberries are related to roses. Just takes a demonstration of their relative thorny powers to see the family resemblance.

They are all pricks.

The sun barely eked over a small verdant valley when Tyb and I trudged up a hill and into his house. I was so wiped out that as soon as he led me to a small room he declared mine, I fell on the bed and passed out, shoes still on. Now bright eyed and bushy tailed, I took in my surroundings. My room possessed a full-size bed topped with a faded quilt. On the wall with the door, a large built-in bookcase filled with reading material. Opposite of the door was a large window with a small chaise lounge situated in the center. Between the chaise and bed, not much walking space.

As I stood up and stretched again, Tyb popped his head in the door. "Let me give you the tour. I already milked the goats and cow, so I'll show you how at the night milking."

So thus it began. First the twenty-five cent tour of the house. Between my bedroom and Tyb's chamber lurked the bathroom. Not just any bathroom, mind you. This was special in a way I couldn't even begin to describe. Composting toilet? I did not know one could compost crap, but there it goes to show my ignorance. After each use of the privy, I was instructed to toss a scoop of a mixture in a bucket on top of my waste. That, Tyb told me, would help the bacteria break down, contain odor, and generate quality compost to be used in the garden.

"Say what now? You're going to put shit on food crops? Nasty!" Ewww. Way eww.

"It's *humanure* and it's not shit when it gets applied to the soil. The heat from composting two years kills the pathogens. It's safe, when handled correctly. I didn't want to risk contaminating my aquifer if an earthquake should happen and the septic tank crack, leaking into the groundwater. Isn't as fancy as running water, but it works."

The bathtub and pedestal sink looked normal enough. We left the bathroom. To the left, Tyb's room. In front of me, the living area. Wide, open. The house faced south, and that southern exposure was channeled into a great atrium sort of thing. A whole room of nothing but plants in leafy splendor. It was separated from the living area by a glass wall. On the east side of the great room, the kitchen. Dividing the living area and the cooking area, a massive bench thing, at least seven feet long and five feet high at the tallest point. The end facing the atrium had a square hole with a bunch of twigs sticking out, and a large upside down barrel behind the aperture. .

"That's my rocket mass heater. It's my central heating."

"I've never seen anything like it." Behind the barrel, the rocket mass heater had a bench for sitting upon, as Tyb demonstrated.

"This thing is epic. Doesn't produce any smoke."

Color me impressed. The kitchen seemed out of suburbia. Tyb took me outside, through the atrium. The view from his front door was the stuff of travel posters. A mountainous view rife with conifers, wildflowers, and ferns. Below, the hillside gave way to a meadow. On the right side of the meadow, Tyb pointed out a group of earth-berm buildings set against the trees and hidden to a casual eye, with greenery growing wild on the little hillocks.

"That's the cackleberry coop, over there is the milking shed. I pasture raise my stock—except for the rabbits—so there's not much in the way of mucking things out." As he spoke, he strode down the little pathway leading towards the henhouse. "I do the deep litter method for the chickens. Once a week, we'll spread a layer of pine needles in the coop. It kills the smell, and as it composts, it helps keep the chickens warm. It's important because it gets wicked cold here in the winter." Tyb opened coop's door and showed me the impressive eight-inch depth of composting chicken crap. He was right, though. It didn't stink at all in the chicken house. Tyb then led me to the milking shed. It was whitewashed on the inside, with a long wooden stool in the center. The stool had a U shaped doo-hickie at one end sticking up, the two sides of the U held together with a little chain. "That's the milking stanchion. Give each goat a nice scoop of oats. Keeps them calm while you get the goods." Tyb pointed to a galvanized garbage can in the corner. "Always make sure the lid is on that tight, otherwise chipmunks and squirrels steal it all. They are fuzzy, bucktoothed thieves."

I nodded. Makes sense, the furry rat-bastards. Wasn't sure exactly how to milk a goat, but I could totally bribe one, no problem. My tour guide whisked me away, back up to the house. "Okay, what I'm about to show you, stays between you, me and Zamara." We walked back through the greenhouse and into the living quarters. Tyb walked to his room, opened the door and flicked on a light. "I use solar cells with a backup bio-diesel-powered generator for electricity. But things can and will go wrong. If we are ever in a situation where you need to hide, here's the place to duck." Tyb's room was masculine and had the scent of leather and soap. A huge bedstead hewn from logs took up most of the room, a worn quilt covering the bed. One side had a dresser with photos on top. The far side of the room had an L-shaped computer desk. Tyb walked to the desk and fell to his knees, crawling under the big piece of furniture, reaching for the very corner of the room. He pressed something, and then a small door swung open. The door was about two feet tall and three foot wide. One couldn't see it from the door because the desk blocked the view. Tyb crawled through, saying, "Follow me."

I hunkered down on all fours and did as he did. The passageway was cool and gently downward sloping. "Where does this go?" I asked, exhilarated to be in an actual secret passage. Would this be a *Being John Malkovich* moment?

"Two exits. If you stay to the left and follow the path, it'll take you to the far end of the meadow. There's a shortcut there to where I store my cars. If you go to the right, it'll take you to the panic room."

"You have a panic room out here?" Whew, not the New Jersey turnpike.

"I live my life on the interesting side. I'd rather have one and never use it, than not having one when I need it most."

"Regular boy scout, aren't you?"

"Nope. Couldn't stand the merit badge sash."

"I would have taken you for the type to tightly roll your kerchief."

"Nope, it was the sash."

We crawled along in the dark, when Tyb spoke up. "Go right."

"Aye, aye captain."

The path evened out and it wasn't long before Tyb stood up in front of me. I got to my feet, and tried to hear what he was doing. Only a moment passed before I heard the unlatching of a door. Then a light turned on, blinding me. So this is what Gizmo felt when he cried "bright light!" in agony.

I used a hand to shade my eyes. Could see Tyb was doing the same, as he stood in a small room, about ten foot square. There was a cot and shelves holding things marked MRE. "No one knows this room is here, except you and my sister. If you ever get freaked and need to hide, come in here, bolt that door. There's a walkie talkie in that plastic tote, the other is in the kitchen."

"Where does that door go?" I pointed to the door facing

the entry Tyb and I used.

"That goes to the treehouse."

"Treehouse?" Oh, so Zamara wasn't jesting, like I hoped.

"Actually, it's a fake tree house. Looks like a tree, but it's reinforced concrete, tinted. Looks like an ancient stump. That door goes to the treehouse, which would be the equivalent of a castle's keep. It's like this room, but bigger. Made to withstand a siege."

"Why would you feel the need to construct such a thing?" My mind was officially blown. This man before me carved out his own kingdom from the wilderness. Seemed fairly efficient to me, but being ignorant in all things rural, my opinion really doesn't mean much.

"Oh, when I was a teenager, I broke the heart of a girl. Her daddy didn't like me, he had connections. Some of his douchemonkey relatives tried knocking me out of the picture."

"Overkill much? You were a teenager."

"Yeah, but a newspaper heading about what an sexually abusive fuck he was to his own daughter because I narked to the cops about him being a piece of shit... Well, her father pretty much wanted to bathe in my blood."

"Why would he do such a thing?"

"He was a senator and loved exercising his power over others. I refused to be another of his pawns."

I quieted, not sure what to say. Didn't matter though. Tyb spoke up before I could form a thought. "Come on, Izzy. I'm pretty sure you wouldn't mind a nice bath and something to eat. I just noticed you're in the same clothes as last night. As for the last time my sister fed you, if she's anything like she used to be, food isn't high on her priority list."

"That is true." And deep underground, I looked upon the man who was keeping me safe from another abusive fuck. He had closely cropped curly black hair, like his sister. But his eyes were an amber color and fringed with thick lashes. His eyebrows weren't huge, but well defined and framed his gaze. Tyb stood about six inches taller than I, well-built with a muscular frame. He'd have to be all muscle, considering the lifestyle he lives. In the moment I studied him closely, I noticed him studying me back. "How do I measure up?"

He cleared his throat before replying with a half-smile. "We'll see when you grope a goat."

Great. Interspecies nipple play. Yeah.

This will be interesting.

Chapter Ten

You know what's a thousand hues of awesome? A hot bubble bath in a huge tub. What's even better than that? Knowing Christos isn't around to hold my head under water.

I lounged in the tub for over an hour. Tyb patiently tolerated my mermaid time. The time spent in the tub was utilized in rumination of my wicked change of circumstances. My naivety had me here, in the mountains, away from family. I chose not to write my parents. My mom can't lie to save her face and my dad wouldn't be able to keep his cool and resist the urge for open Christos season. Maybe when things settle down, I'll contact them, but I dared not to write. I didn't want to underestimate Christos and his tenacity for getting what he wants.

I thought about Tyb. He seemed infinitely capable, like his sister. Intelligent, too. In a way, I deeply admired his homestead. I mean, it's quite the accomplishment to literally build one's home with bare hands, raise and tend stock, grow feed for people and animals. Everything gets reused, everything is orderly, and everything has a logical reason for being the way it is. There is no convenience out here—if I want Starbucks, tough shit. Go shopping? Ha. Watch TV? Not happening. He at least had a computer with satellite access to the internet. However, that link to the outside world happens to reside in Tyb's bedroom, and I'm not terribly keen on asking for visitation with high-technology, not at this point. Tyb is an intriguing man, I would admit. Tried thinking about Christos living the rural, hardworking life. Pretty sure he'd rather swing by his neck from a tree than milk a goat or shovel chicken poop himself. If money can't solve Christos' problem, then he gets mad and acts out. Living a homesteading existence would be torture to him.

The thing that coaxed me from the watery refuge was the scent of breakfast cooking. Had no idea what time it was, but food sounded so good. After getting out of the tub, I wrapped a huge towel around me and ducked back into my room. My suitcase went the way of the Blackberry Christos gave me, and the sports car Tyb provided as a fiery diversion. I had most of the clothes I bought on my spree, some boots and underpinnings. Most of my Lush haul made it through, too. If I am to be exiled to the middle of nowhere for years, then damn yes, I'm keeping my pampering goods. No doubt in my mind that I'd need their healing properties. But most everything, including my purse, got chucked over that cliff side.

I put on some clean jeans, a tee shirt, lightweight wool socks, and my boots. Ran a brush through my hair and tried tying it back into a ponytail. Forgot I got a Meg Ryan-type pixie cut. With a deep breath, I walked toward what was sure to be the first of many mornings spent in this manner.

"What's for breakfast, Chef?"

"Eggs, bacon, and toast."

"Bacon? You didn't mention any pigs."

Tyb laughed. "It's nice that you think I raise swine, too. I don't though. Neighbor down the hill does, and he does them well. We barter rabbit pelts for pig parts."

"So you raise the rabbits for their fur?" I tried not to cringe at the thought of all those bunnies, awaiting their fate as underwear lining or a fur coat.

"No, their meat. Fur is a by-product someone else can utilize and I can benefit from."

"You eat rabbit?" That's like maybe two steps above road kill, right?

"Yep. All sorts of cute critters. They taste adorable." Tyb cracked a smirk.

"But it's a rabbit." I grew up with a pet bunny named FooFooBunns. She liked to cuddle on my shoulder and hide in my hair. Could never have eaten or worn my sweet FoofyBunBunny. That's like cannibalism.

"And a lamb is just a baby, but that doesn't stop the manufacturing of mint jelly or the legs of said lambs showing up at the grocery store, does it? Anyhow, I'm letting you decide what's next after breakfast, shooting or showing you the boundaries of the property."

I bet shooting involves a lot less hiking. "Shooting. Best be on the safe side."

"Will do. I'd like for you to get proficient with the firearm with both hands. That way, if your usual hand is impaired, your safety is not. We'll start off with a sidearm. Eventually, we'll work you up to a shotgun and rifle, if you decide to go trekking."

"Trekking?" With all the animals, I assumed Tyb stayed close to home.

"Yep. There's a nice lake about five hours hike from here. I like to set up the automatic feeders and let the dogs handle keeping things on lockdown. Go camping for a night, come back."

When Tyb mentioned dogs, I immediately thought of the pup that howled like a banshee to wake me up. "Where's the little dog with the aristocratic title?"

"Lady Dunklebee? She's somewhere."

At the sound of her name, the dog came trotting from the atrium to stand next to Tyb and give me the canine equivalent of the Stink Eye. "Ah, there she is."

"What breed is she?" Cute, I'll admit. Red and white, with perked ears that spread like butterfly wings.

"She's a Papillion. Member of the spaniel family."

"And the big dogs…?"

"Are strictly outside, working dogs. Lady Dunklebee is a companion mutt, although she shuns people most of the time."

So, I'd be making acquaintance with several dogs. Okay, never really been around them, but I could adjust. "Are they friendly?"

"It's not their job to be friendly. But if I introduce you to them, they won't see you as a threat. Let them sniff your hand. I'll have you start feeding them when you go to collect the eggs."

My mental checklist of the chores I needed to do kept growing. I didn't mind, staying busy is important, but Tyb wasn't joking when he said he'd drop a lot of knowledge on me today.

Tyb slid a plate of breakfast my way, as I sat down at the table nestled between the rocket mass heater and the wall in the back of the kitchen. "Coffee or tea?"

"Coffee, please."

With a tea kettle in one hand, and a cone-shaped-linen-lined sieve situated in a little wooden stand, Tyb began to pour the boiling water into the contraption with a coffee cup below the sieve, to catch the magical elixir of vitality. The smell of coffee perfumed the room.

"Non-electric coffee maker?" I couldn't resist asking.

"Damn skippy. Best cup of coffee you will drink, I promise."

I took him for his word, as he handed me a steaming cup of joe. Perhaps it was the deprivation of caffeine which made me appreciate the drink more. Took a sip. Smooth as silk and utterly delicious. Time on the clock said it wasn't even ten a.m. which I found hard to believe. What time did he wake me up? "Are these Kona beans?"

"Nope. No fancy beans here. Just stuff out of a tin can."

Color me amazed. As I got down to business of chowing down on breakfast, Tyb turned on a radio. Turned on, being technical jargon for cranking the handle on the radio's side before turning it physically on. A commercial hit my ears. Seemed out of place because of the quiet of Tyb's home. After the commercial break, and just in the moment I was shoving a forkful of eggs into my gob, a female newscaster made a breaking report.

"This just in: Correspondents in Berkeley, California, report a series of explosions located at the newly-opened Haytham Laboratory shaking the city this morning. Lead scientist and entrepreneur, Christos Haytham is reported to have been in the building when the first fireball engulfed the industrial neighborhood which housed the laboratory. At this time, no one knows how the fire started. Emergency personnel have been dispatched from surrounding East Bay cities to fight the inferno. On another sad note, Jakob Haytham's wife, Selesta Ferrous-Haytham has been reported missing with her body guard. Mrs. Ferrous-Haytham was reported to be returning home after the opening of her husband's new laboratory. The body guard's car and various personal items have been located, however the bodies have not been found. The coast guard have several patrol boats searching the area. Haytham's press agents have no comment for us at this time." Tyb turned off the radio and faced me.

"You failed to mention some things to me. You and my sister both." I gulped. The accusatory tone didn't foretell of a happy thought. "You. *You are Selesta.*"

Couldn't lie. It's upon this man's good will that I have a safe place to hide. "Yes." I held his gaze while I replied. "I am Selesta Elizzybeth Ferrous-Haytham."

Quietly, he asked, "Why didn't Zamara tell me?"

"I don't know why, she just said I should keep it to myself until you warm up to me."

"Well, yeah. Fuck Jakob Christos Haytham in his goddamn ear with a fucking shard of glass. I hate that fucker."

"Why?" His anger toward my deception was nothing compared to the ire unleashed by mentioning my insane husband's name.

"His uncle is the fucknut senator, as in the senator's daughter, Haytham's cousin is my ex-girlfriend. Christos *MotherFucking Haytham* tried killing me because law enforcement began investigating the senator for child abuse and he had ambitions of the White House. My goddamn treehouse is because of that son of a bitch, and now I have his wife? Fucking A, what's next, a nuclear apocalypse?" He gave a short bark of a laugh at what I assumed must be the absurdity of it all.

I swallowed hard. "Yeah, you might want to call your sister and ask her what Virteria Serum is… because according to her, that's a very real possibility. And from the psychotic babble coming from my husband's lips, she was right."

Chapter Eleven

I looked down the revolver's barrel and thought about my husband. A fire. Blown up? Dead? Scarred for life? How does the lab going boom change my life? How did the fire start? Did he have something to do with it? Couldn't, he loved that lab more than me…

"Izzy, you aren't focusing on the task at hand. Stay in the moment." Tyb's voice caressed my ear as he stood behind me, giving instruction on gun safety and technique. "Now, when you have that soda can in your sight, gently squeeze the trigger. There will be a little kick as the combustion from gunpowder pushes the bullet from the barrel. Don't hold your arm locked like that, relax your elbow a little… yeah. Perfect. Take your shot when you're ready."

A deep breath. Focused my thoughts on nailing that can. Pulled the trigger and POW! A puff of dirt from the hillside right behind the target flew into the air above the can. "Dammit." Dropped my arm holding the heavy gun. Pistols are heavy, I tell you.

"You aimed a little high, Izzy. Picture where you aimed, lower your barrel a tiny bit and try another round. I don't know many people who get bulls eyes the first time they shoot a gun."

I did just that. Aimed a little lower. Pulled the trigger and the can ended up flying. "I did it! I killed the can!"

Tyb laughed. "That's a start, Izzy. Moving targets get exponentially harder. By the way, if you are on the receiving end of gunfire, run in a serpentine pattern."

"Umm, okay. Good to know." Really hope that bit of advice is unneeded though.

Tyb walked from behind me to my side. "Life is unpredictable at best. If push comes to shove, and you need to defend yourself, never aim an unloaded weapon at a person. If that person is irrefutably after your life, you fucking shoot them. Gut shot to incapacitate, then a head shot. Never give them an opportunity to come after you again. You shoot, you shoot to kill."

This was heavy stuff. I mean, I totally get what he's saying and why, but could I kill someone? Even in self-defense? I have a hard time picturing myself doing so, in that fashion. But who knows what would happen if shit hits the fan. "Duly noted."

"I don't mean to freak you out, Izzy, I really don't. But you have to be prepared for when shit gets real. If this were the middle ages, you would know where to hide when the raiders come. If you were male, you would've been required to master the long bow, if you were English, that is. My point is that what was once common sense is now a vague ideal to most. In this day and age, the vast majority of people won't experience war on a first hand basis—and the news doesn't count. We've become out of touch with the animal within us all. That said, everyone deserves a fighting chance. By learning to protect yourself, you are getting that opportunity." His warm brown eyes held my own for a long moment. "This is not the same world you are used to. Can't say it plainer than that. My sister says you're important. Zamara is many things; liar is not one of them."

Was Tyb a survivalist, like that one guy from the movie, *Tremors*? At any rate, we don't live in a time when warfare strikes the nation. We're beyond that sort of mentality. Deflect time. "Why do you still call me Izzy? You know my real name."

Without missing a beat, Tyb replied, "Selesta died when her body guard's car careened off that cliff. You are *not* her, you do *not* live her life, nor are you likely to see many people from that incarnation for *quite* some time. I see no reason to call you who you are not."

Well, that solves that burning question. "Okie doke. Good point." I needed to get into the mindset of not being me. Perhaps I shouldn't have chosen Izzy as my name, since Izzy is a play on Lizzy. My mother bestowed my middle name with *Lizzy*, after the Beatles song, *Dizzy Miss Lizzy*. "So, is Tyb your whole name? Curious minds want to know."

He crossed his arms and spoke. "My name, since you must know, is Tybias. Couldn't stand it as a kid. So, anyways, moving on. Remember how to safety the weapon?"

I nodded and showed him by flipping the safety on the gun so it couldn't accidentally fire.

"Holster your sidearm and let's go meet the goats. Want them to love you? Give 'em some treats."

Okay. Super goatie time. "What kind of treats?"

"Sweet ones. Wait and see."

I was right, shooting involved less hiking. On the north side of the hill house, a sturdy three-sided lean-to thingie housed the Mule. We piled in and away we went. Not a long drive, but a hilly one, with Tyb fishtailing around muddy corners. It was kinda fun. The return ride was just the same.

On the other side of the milking shed, hidden within the forest, lurked the hilly domain of goats. A large paddock enclosed their grazing area. Some were black and brown, a couple solid black.

As we strode toward the gate, Tyb educated me on his milkers. "The two-color ones are Oberhasli goats. They make the bulk of my dairy operation. The black ones are Mercia-Granada. They have high milk-fat. That milk-fat makes for awesome cheese and butter."

"Good to know. And they get milked twice a day?"

"Yep. When I need them freshened, I do artificial insemination. Billy goats stink, and the smell can taint the milk. With AI, I can get quality goats with quality milk and no off-flavors."

"What do you do with all the cheese?"

"Eat it. If I make extra, I smoke it. Cheese fondue in the middle of winter is a truly splendid thing."

I nodded. Could easily imagine this mountain of his getting snowed in during winter. Having preserved foods would be a good thing. Donner party type of catering? No thanks and not likely.

"Do you can stuff, too?" Couldn't resist asking just how much he preps for winter.

"Why yes, yes I do. Pretty much everything. That way I'm not dependent on a freezer or electricity to keep my food safe. Oh! After the goats, I'll show you the root cellar."

"Root cellar?" I think my grandparents had one at their house. Or maybe it was a storm cellar? It was something cellar, that much I know.

"Yep. Potatoes, carrots, onions and canned goods."

Okay. I keep adding things onto my mental map of the property. This is what early cartographers must have felt like, ever tweaking their charts the further they journeyed.

Tyb opened the gate and held it wide for me, then locked it again once I was inside. As soon as the goats saw him, they began to baa like sheep and crowd around, nuzzling his hands. "My greedy girls looking for some treats? Oh, alright… Just for you sweeties."

I smiled at the crooning baby-talk voice Tyb used. He walked to the milking shed, went inside and popped back out with an industrial sized container of peanut butter and a huge handful of wooden spoons. The goats caught sight of him and crowded around, bumping each other to be first in line to get the goods.

"Want to see something funny?"

I nodded, eagerly anticipating this show.

Tyb popped open the peanut butter container, tucked it under his arm and transferred the bulk of spoons to the now-free hand. With his other, he got one spoon and scooped a little peanut butter on it. "Okay girlies. Line up!"

They did and fast. Shoulder to shoulder. This was obviously not their first rodeo. Now that they were lined up, Tyb took the spoon and planted the handle in the earth, peanut butter in the air. Goat one got her treat. He repeated the gesture for each of the goats, who each demolished the dollop of peanut buttery goodness presented.

After giving the last goat her treat, he capped the peanut butter tub and bent down. "Come here, take a look."

I knelt by his side and gandered at what he wanted to show me.

"Okay, I'll school you on this now so later we can get right down to business." He gestured at the goat's hind end. "This is the udder. Those are the teats. The objective is to mimic a kid, baby goat that is, and get the milk. Make the 'OK!' sign with your hand."

I did, curving my index finger to touch my thumb, splaying my other fingers out.

"Good. You'll encircle the teat with that loop you made, as close to the udder as you can get. You'll cradle the teat in your hand and then squeeze gently, starting top to bottom. Repeat as needed until the goat is dry." Tyb reached up and patted the goat's back. "They are pretty tolerant, but for the first milking or two, I'll be handy. After that, you'll be on your own."

I took a deep breath and tried calming my insides. There was nothing prurient in how he explained milking a goat, nor did he use a *bow-chicka-wow* voice. Everything he said was matter of fact.

But for some odd reason, I couldn't shake the notion of Tyb's hands groping my tits.

Chapter Twelve

The rest of the day flew by pretty quickly. After meeting the goats, I was introduced to the root cellar. It was next to the lean-to, built as an earth berm building, with a large wooden door bolted from the outside. When opened, it revealed a large room, lined with shelves. And then shelving ran down the center, anchored by at the floor and ceiling. Everything was packed. Quart jars, pint jars and everything in between, all organized by content and secured in its spot with elastic strapping.

"That way if I get in an earthquake, things will rattle but not fall."

Awesome.

There were bins situated below shelves on the left side of the room. The bins were mostly empty of their vegetables. Come fall, they would be full again, to last the year.

After locking up the root cellar, Tyb turned around and whistled loud and clear for a long moment. Then silence. A minute passed. Then the sound of thundering paws. A herd of huge white dogs and two smaller, colorful dogs made their presence known.

"These are my helpers. The white ones are Maremmas. Biggest is RiffRaff." That dog came to Tyb when he said its name, and Tyb petted the massive dog on the head. "Back to work, Riff." Dog trotted off. "He watches the chickens. Next biggest is Frank N. Furter, on patrol duty."

I quirked my brow at that revelation. Okay…

Each dog came as their name was mentioned, and each dog was dismissed with a, 'back to work'. The other Maremmas were Magenta (goats), Colombia (goats), and Eddie (patrol). The other dogs were Australian Shepard's with bright blue eyes and mottled coats. "These are my goat herders, Brad and Janet."

"So, *Rocky Horror Picture Show* fan?"

"Can't say fan, but I am fond of the whole idea. That, and Tim Curry is my favorite actor of all time."

The more I spoke to Tyb, the more I liked what I saw. Feelings of confusion pounded my mind. I didn't want to explore that avenue, not yet. I got suckered in by Christos because I was naïve. Now, I'm a little wiser, I hope. Tyb could have a huge flaw that I don't know about, and eyehumping the man simply because he wasn't Christos, isn't a smart thing to do. I made a stupid compromise with myself. I could think about Tyb being tawdry, but not act on it. Not until I know him better. Jumping into bed with the first guy to make my pulse quicken taught me a very important lesson: vaginas can be fun, but using one to replace thorough thought is bad. *Very, very, bad.* It's not my fault that Tyb's callused hands were sexy in a way I never experienced before. This was a man who could build a mountain with his bare hands, if given enough time and material. Christos seemed like a prissy boy compared to Tyb's rock hard manliness.

Dammit! My train of lustful thought derailed as Tyb asked me something about parsnips.

"I'm sorry, what?"

"Are you fond of parsnips?"

I shrugged my shoulders. "Never had one."

"Can't believe how deprived you were in your former life."

"Terrible, isn't it?"

"Must have been, else you wouldn't be here."

"Touché, sir, touché."

"Are you always this funny?"

"No, not always. But I don't think you're going to start whaling on me for being a smart ass."

"Your husband did that?"

I bit my lip and started walking around the hill to make for the house. I didn't want to talk about Christos, especially to someone who held a huge grudge already. It's too easy to get on the pity me train, and I really didn't want my ticket stamped for that trip. "Let's just say my husband did a lot of not cool things."

"I'm sorry. I shouldn't have asked." Tyb sounded genuinely contrite for posing the query.

I stopped and turned around to face him. "I don't have a problem with you asking. Especially since I know I'm not the only victim at his hands. Christos did a lot of things to me, both physical, mental and emotional. Right now, I'm not sure what the worst was. But yeah. I wasn't allowed to have an opinion. He didn't want me to even buy my own clothes alone or drive myself to the doctor. He wanted utter and complete control over me. Felt like I was a heroine of some eighties historical romance novel, where she gets abducted and immersed in a seductive and dangerous world, with a master who wants to own her body and soul. It's smothering. Had to constantly walk on egg shells. Never wanted to say something that would upset him or otherwise cast a cloud on an otherwise sunny day for him. Every time he opened his mouth to speak to me, I usually thought 'oh shit…!' and wondered when the other foot was about to drop. That's not healthy. That's not good for a person. Then all of a sudden, he started talking about how I'd be mother to a new world and how I'm worthy to bear his seed… It really creeped me out. That, Tyb, is why I ran. Either I get away or I get killed. And I really have no doubt that if I angered him enough, he would kill me in a rage. I am absolutely certain of that."

"What makes you so sure?"

I swallowed hard, thinking of that bastard's words in San Francisco. "Because he told me less than a week ago, that if I ever betrayed him, he knew exactly where he'd hide my body."

Tyb's expression darkened. "That's a shitty thing to say. I hope you don't take offense, but I'm glad you decided to run. It's hard to turn your back on everything you know and go forth not knowing that the future holds, but it's a braver thing than sitting in a shitty relationship, wondering if today is the day they snap and you die."

I smiled a little at Tyb, and resumed walking to the house. Dammit. He's too easy to like. "So, how long have you been in exile up here?"

"Almost seventeen years."

Wow. "Really? And no social life other than your family and the strays your sister drags over?" Stopped halfway up the hill to the house and faced him again.

Tyb grinned. "Nope, no life, other than running this homestead. Takes too long to run down the mountain and hang out at the bar in town, hoping to meet an eligible barfly with a penchant for animal husbandry. Besides, from my limited understanding, women are trouble. Voodoo vaginas and things like that."

I burst out laughing at his mention of *voodoo vaginas*. "What about the magic penises can do, being the built-in wand of torment?"

"I'm pretty sure female nether regions hold more power. It's why they have the power to carry children. It's a more potent magic."

"So be it. Not going to argue."

"Are you capitulating because I'm right or because you just don't want to debate?"

"You have a valid point, but without genetic contribution from a male, our species would quickly die out."

"Well, here's to the species not dying out anytime soon. Side note, I'm actually glad you're here. It's nice to have a conversation with someone who talks back. Lady Dunklebee is great for snuggling, but not so wonderful at witty conversation."

"Duly noted. Besides, I'm sure it's more than my sparkling wit that makes you happy to have me around." Let it be because I make him smirk and because I am capable, when given instruction and encouragement without fear.

"You're right. It's great to have someone around to help out. Things will get done faster since I'm not shouldering it alone."

"Yay, working for room and board!" My sarcasm was starting to get warmed up.

Tyb replied, "Yay, pretty girl stranded out here for company!" and grinned.

I could feel my face flame.

Shit and awesome. He thinks I'm pretty, even half muddy and shorn like a sheep.

Decided to brazen out the banter. "Yay, stranded out in the middle of nowhere with a guy who thinks I'm purty!"

"Funny, too. Modest, even." Tyb dropped the laughing face and spoke low. "I'm almost sure Mara is punishing me for pulling the heads off all her Barbies as kids."

"Why is that?" My curiosity stoked at his words.

Tyb looked me in the eyes and I felt as though he was staring through me and able to see the attraction I had for him. "Because it's been a very long time since I've been graced with the company of someone so interesting."

"Interesting, eh? Why am I interesting."

"Because you are an attractive female adept at banter. It's a nice change of pace, and the view isn't so bad, either. You can stop biting your lip, Izzy. In fact, if you could refrain from biting your lip, at least when I can see you, it'd be great."

I was puzzled. "Sorry. It's a force of habit thing."

"No, it's okay. Just gives me thoughts I shouldn't entertain about someone I don't want to touch."

Before I could reign in my tongue, I asked rather indignantly, "Why don't you want to touch me?" Here I've been, trying not to picture Tyb's hands caressing my body and naked fun time, exhilarated by his admission that he found me attractive. He stating he didn't want to touch me was very much cold water on my delusions of possible seduction down the line, if I found him really worthwhile.

With a leery look, Tyb said only two words with the expectation that I would know exactly what he meant. "*Voodoo vagina.*"

Chapter Thirteen

Voodoo Vagina. Voodoo Vagina. Voodoo Vagina...

That little mantra echoed in my mind for close to a minute before I started snickering like a dipshit high on laughing gas.

"What is so funny?" Tyb demanded. I bet he was perplexed that I went from solidly dumbfounded to giggling dip in under sixty.

"I was thinking that if I ever started a jazz trio, I'm going to call it *Voodoo Vagina*. In the liner notes of the first album, there'll be an acknowledgment to you." You know, this bodes well. Tyb is so refreshingly upfront; it felt like a stimulating breeze after the stagnant swamp of Christos' dancing around topics.

Tyb started laughing. "You know, we're almost finished with day one, and I'm not sure whether to be thrilled or scared shitless."

"Please, be thrilled. I don't want to clean up diarrhea, thank you very much."

"If I make the mess, I clean it up. First rule of homesteading."

"Seems almost too logical."

"That's because I watch a lot of Star Trek on YouTube. Spock and his logic." Tyb started walking past me on the raspberry-lined pathway to the front door. "My mind was blown when Mara gave me a computer and smartphone for Christmas. She arranged with some guy she was dating to hook me up with piggy-backed satellite internet. She showed me three websites: Google, Wikipedia, and YouTube. Think I spent three days surfing the net before I got over it."

"That must have been like culture shock." I started walking again to keep pace with him. "Especially the smartphone."

"Hell yes! I came up here in 1996. Only doctors and drug dealers had cell phones, and they weren't some futuristic doo-dad one touched like in a sci-fi movie."

We reached the door, and Tyb held it open for me. "Thank you, sir." I walked into the indoors jungle, eyeing the lush growth. One side was edibles, or at least edibles I recognized. Tomatoes, peppers, cabbage, lettuce and other salad fixings. The other side, an undecipherable forest.

"Anytime, ma'am." He walked towards the kitchen, to stop at the sink and wash his hands. Then Tyb progressed to wrangling lunch. I headed toward the bathroom.

Once inside, I relieved myself and at the sink, studied my reflection in the oval mirror. I kinda liked the pixie cut, spikey and windblown. Being in the sun would lighten my hair. I'm okay with that. Had circles beneath my eyes and attributed that to last night's flight. Holy shit, was that only last night? Felt so disconnected with everything, and now with Tyb being way too attractive for either of our good... Confusion, oh the damned confusion! Divorce carries over in a new life, right? I'm free and clear, right? In my awakening against Christos' abuse, I emotionally divorced him. I started biting my lip in vexation and stopped. *Sigh.* Play everything by ear. New world. No need to over think things. I'll listen to my gut this time instead of rationalizing everything away.

When Tyb discovered who I was, his anger melted away almost as fast as it appeared. He didn't menace, didn't growl. He got sarcastic and accepted what it was and moved on.

Wish I could have met him in my past life...

I washed my hands and ventured towards the kitchen. There was a lot of stainless steel. Sink, stove, fridge. I suspect though, they were chosen more for utility than aesthetics. Light wood cabinetry held everything, while dark burl wood countertops finished it. "Where did you get your countertops?"

Tyb stood at the stove, spatula in hand while he tended what looked to be grilled cheese sandwiches. "Got them here."

"You made them?"

He never turned around to speak, just focused on the sandwiches. "Yep. I lived in a tent for six months, then a little cabin I built in time for winter. Once that was done, I started growing things—animals and crops. About ten years into living in that one-roomed cabin, got stir crazy and started clearing the land. My sister would visit all summer long, she helped to frame this house. She even brought a bunch of books about building green. Took a couple years to finish the house – we only framed, roofed and walled the outside that summer. Made buddies with the sheriff—and his friend with a helicopter license, coincidentally. We were going to airlift the glass panels into the valley here, but couldn't. A dead tree was going all leaning Tower of Pisa, and we had to cut it down to give clearance—and there was no way I was going to let the helicopter land in my garden. So, we cut it down and boom, here's this huge chunk of art. It made the countertops, the toilet seat and lid, that table there, a couple chairs… every scrap got used, really."

"Good to have friends in high places, eh?"

"Yep, it is good. Good to have family in higher places, though."

I smiled when he put late lunch in front of me. "Where did you learn to cook?"

"Used to watch Great Chefs of PBS after school. Julia Child, too. Watched and applied. Seems to work."

I bit into the buttery yet crisp bread cradling cheese of melting-goodness. "Honestly, with all you've shown me, I'm a bit intimidated."

"Don't be. There's only eight goats, so milking doesn't take very long. All the milk gets stored in the springbox until Saturday. That's the day I make cheese and butter. Eggs get collected every day, but again, that doesn't take long. Fifteen minutes tops. In regards to the crops, the real hard work is at planting and at harvest. Otherwise, all it really takes is water—and that's negated by the hugelbeds I built, so I don't really have to water them that much. If everything is set up well to begin with, then really, it's just a matter of keeping it running well. I grow mainly perennials, that way I don't have to reseed everything every year. The main thing really, is the grain. But that's two days of harvest, a couple days of drying, then threshing. Everything is on a seasonal clock. That makes a huge difference."

The more he spoke, the more impassioned he grew about his lifestyle choice. I don't know if I could make it one season, let alone several years.

"I'll do my best, Tyb. But I wasn't in FFA or 4H. This is total foreign territory."

"That's okay, Izzy. You're learning, that's the important part. I could flap my lips and you not listen… That's when we'd have an issue. That's not the case, so I'm more than willing to be patient. Hey, want a beer with your lunch?"

"You have beer up here?"

"I *make* beer up here." Satisfaction soaked his voice.

"Yes, I will have one." Cold beer sounds good.

"Do you have any objections to me turning the radio back on?"

"None whatsoever." Actually, I was very curious to find out what was known about Christos and his situation. If they found his body, I would be free. Could donate the bulk of his wealth to charities and just go on, forging my way. It'd be too easy, though.

Tyb wound up the radio and switched it on. Then the world changed.

"Pure anarchy is ruling the Bay Area. After Haytham Labs suffered a series of explosions, HAZMAT teams from across the region were called in to contain the area. After being declared a Federal Disaster Area, all traffic into and out of the city has been halted as a quarantine mandate has been issued. Officials are quiet on the source of contamination, but experts from UC Berkeley are chiming in with various theories. Everything from comet dust to nuclear fallout has been proposed. Rescuers are still searching for survivors in the ruins, although the likelihood is slim, according to fire science experts."

"Switch the station, Tyb."

He fiddled with the dial, and after a moment of static, a voice faded in. "While officials are not sure what caused the fireball to expand at such a rate, well over a fifty-mile radius has been affected by the snow-like particulate matter falling from the sky. Residents of California, north to south, are encouraged to stay indoors and wear a respiratory mask when going outside."

Again, Tyb fiddled with the radio's dial and found a new station. This one scared me most of all. I knew that voice. Hoped never to hear it, let alone listen to the insanity spewing forth. My eyes never left Tyb's as that voice of evil sank into my brain and chilled my bones.

"And when I find that lying bitch, I will skin her alive. No one leaves me. *No one.* Selesta, your ass is mine. When I find you, you lying cunt, you will learn who is master of their universe. You were my wife. No more. Now you are the hunted. Skin you. Skin you. Skin you...."

Chapter Fourteen

Tyb and I both jumped when his cell phone rang. The ringtone he had sounded like an old rotary phone, and it killed the silence between the radio, Tyb and I.

He answered the call, relief washing over his face. "Hey, wench… Yeah, we've settled in nicely. What's up with the shit I'm hearing on the radio?...You're fucking kidding me… Fuck… What do you want me to do?... That's it? Seriously? Bucky would love to get in on that action… Fine, your call…. Can do… Okay, see you in three days. Oh, and Mara? I have a hell of a question for you. Why would Christos Haytham's voice be heard on the radio, no more than five minutes ago? … He was talking mad shit about what he'd do to Selesta…" Tyb flashed his eyes at me before looking away and speaking to his sister. "Skin her… yeah. Uh, let me check…" He looked at the station dial on the radio. "101.9…. No, no, no. Don't tell me that sort of shit, sister of mine. Fuck me not." Tyb ran a frustrated hand through his black hair. "Okay. Will do. Three days, no more. Otherwise we're on full fucking lockdown… Got it. See you." Tyb ended the call and looked to me. "Wasn't really going to show you the treehouse unless it became imperative. But it has the tools I need. Mara thinks your husband may have tagged you with a radio chip. Some fancy spy shit. Sub-dermal implant that sends a ping when it's triggered by a FM radio frequency. Can also pirate the radio frequency to broadcast, which is what happened. Haytham has access to a satellite and its feed. So in about twenty minutes he'll get a vague idea where you are when the signal bounces back to him. Which means he's alive and well."

A massive sinking feeling made its presence known in the pit of my stomach. "Seriously? What can we do?" I hoped against hope there was something I could do to prevent that signal from reaching Christos.

"Come on, Izzy. We don't want the ghost of Selesta resurrected." He trotted out the house, and down the path. I followed him, shutting the door behind me.

I quickened my pace to reach his side. "Where we going?"

"Gotta get in the Mule and haul ass to the treehouse. Got no time to spare."

I took that as a challenge and ran full throttle down the winding path, reaching the farm golf-cart before he did. I sat in the seat, hands on the grab bar, eagerly awaiting Tyb to get this clown car going.

He hopped in, started it up and away we went. Good thing I had the grab bar, because skidding through muddy curves on two wheels had me leaning out the side, only to duck back into the cab so tree and brush limbs didn't whack me in the face. There was no trail he drove on as he wended his way through thick forest growth. Five minutes at breakneck speed had us at the base of a massive dead tree in a nearly-empty glade.

Tyb spoke. "Ever see *The Princess Bride*?"

"Uh, yes, only a thousand times." Cary Elwes in a black mask. OMG, yummy. That pirate could pillage my ship any day. Shiver my timbers, even.

"Remember the scene with the albino taking Wesley to the pit of terror? That's kinda like my treehouse."

"A pit of terror?"

"Only for the uninvited." He got out of the Mule and I followed. He walked to a nearby large tree and climbed up, only to reach for a branch. He bent the branch down and then a great rumbling sounded. Tyb let go and fell the six feet to the ground. He whirled around and trotted towards the huge dead tree. "Hurry, it's on a timer!"

Shit. I bolted for Tyb's side, so I would know where the entrance was. The entry point to the treehouse it seems, was at the stump of another dead tree, about twenty feet away. A small door was cracked open. Tyb widened the aperture and stepped inside. "It's amazing what cams, gears, weights, and some chain can do. After pulling that branch, it drops a stone weight which gives slack to the chain holding this door shut. Coring out that tree was a real bitch, by the way. Had to seal it on the inside to keep the sap from gooping shit up. Anyway, the weight falls, and with a series of gears and stuff, the counterweight will pull that door shut again in under thirty seconds. Makes it a pain in the ass for someone who doesn't know that the key goes nowhere near the door." While he spoke, Tyb walked a little ways and started climbing down a ladder. "Come on Izzy, we don't have time to waste."

By now, the door had shut and light, gone. I was in the dark. To play it on the safe side, I crawled on hands and knees toward the ladder Tyb used. It was shorter than I thought. After trotting down a small hallway, things got fancy. Steel door and lights ended the hallway. Tyb already had the door open. There were two other doors in the chamber he stood in. "Come on, Izzy." He opened the left door and lights automatically turned on. The room was Spartan. Chairs surrounding a long table, a bunch of cabinets and shelves, sink and countertop.

"Okay, here, hold this." Tyb put some rectangular gadget in my hand and turned around to dig through some drawers. I looked at the contraption and recognized it as the same Mara used to scan my hotel room. Tyb returned to my side with his hands full of things. Bottles and cotton balls and something wrapped in plastic. When he put it all on the table, I recognized the plastic wrapped items as scalpels in autoclave sterilization packets.

"You're going to cut me?" With Christos' words about skinning me, the thought of something cutting through my flesh did not sit well.

"Sub-dermal means *under skin*. We'll locate it with the wand and I'll remove it. It'll be destroyed."

"Why do you have all this sort of stuff?" Scalpels? Gizmos? *How the hell did he afford all this stuff?*

"Like I mentioned earlier, Haytham tried killing me. Twice. First time, he and his brother beat the shit out of me. Was in the hospital for months. Second time, he ran me off the road. I crashed my car, the hood was smoking when I got out through the passenger side. He didn't see me because he drove on and turned around. By the time he reached my car, it exploded because the fire reached the gas tank. Gave me the chance to disappear off his radar. But in the event he tried finding me again, I was going to be prepared, even if that meant battle-ground surgery."

I swallowed the knot growing in my throat. In my wildest dreams, I could have never conceived my husband doing the things he did before I grew to know the real him. "I'm sorry he caused you to give everything up."

Tyb smirked. "I gave nothing up. I have the world, here. It may not be a fancy city life, but it is more rewarding to me than anything I knew before hand." All business now, he took the gizmo from me and turned it on. "Hold out your arms." I did so, and he scanned them. "Okay, legs." Same thing. "Stand up, please." Can do, and did. First he scanned my front. Lights stayed green on the contraption. "Turn around." I did as asked. No more than ten seconds passed. "Okay, found it."

"Where?" I wanted to know what part of my anatomy Christos branded as his without my knowledge or consent.

"Your, uh, *derriere*."

"Where exactly?"

"What, do you want me to tell you or put your hand there or what?"

"Just touch where it is."

After a short moment, I felt a gentle touch low on my right ass cheek. "It's there."

"Okay. So, what do I need to do, take off my pants?" I turned around to face Tyb, only to notice his cheeks flushed red.

"That would help." He began laying his surgery gear out in a neat and orderly fashion on a paper towel. "I have some lidocaine for the pain." Tyb began to put on latex gloves.

I took a deep breath and tried not thinking about Christos would do if a) he knew I was taking my jeans off in front of a man I found deeply attractive and b) found me. Without Tyb asking, I crawled up onto the table next to his surgery gear and lay face down. If I had known Tyb would be looking at my underwear today, I would have opted for the black lace tanga, instead of my utilitarian cotton bikini.

"Okay, uh, Izzy... I need to, uh, get to the area to numb it.

I'm going to pull your panties down on the right side."

"Do what you have to do, Tyb."

I felt him uncovering my butt cheek for access. "I have a visual on the implant. I'm going to numb the area then remove it the interloper." As soon as he stopped talking, I felt his hand on my ass and then a pinch. "That's the lidocaine." And another pinch. "Two more, okay?"

"Just get the damn thing out of me, Tyb."

Two more pinches and then all I felt was Tyb's hand on my backside. I rather liked it. "Removing implant now." Could feel something happening, but the sensation was hampered by the numb skin. "Okay, got it." He held a small silver and black sliver looking thing with a pair of tweezers and showed it to me. One side was very pointed, and it sickens me to think that one of the times Christos spanked me, he might have implanted that into me, masqueraded as rough love.

Tyb dropped the implant and ground it to pieces beneath his boot heel. "There, and with two minutes to spare." He turned his focus back on my butt. "Okay, let's bandage this up, and you'll be good to go."

I sighed deeply with relief. "So now he won't know where I am."

"In theory. Mara said she'd be here in three days. Hell has broken loose in the Bay Area and it's meandering its way to Sacramento. The whole state will be quarantined before long."

From my spot on the table, I looked up to Tyb. "For how long, I wonder?"

He was busy dabbing some iodine on my incision and putting a guaze pad on the wound. "Don't know. But I'm going to call my sheriff buddy, see what he hears. There. You're done. It's not deep, but we don't want to risk you getting infection." He pulled my underwear up to cover my ass.

I sat up, unnerved by everything going on. Could still hear the echoes of Christos taunting me with skinning as punishment. I took one good look around the room bereft of windows and started crying. Christos will kill me. He'll drag it out and kill me in as painful a way he could devise. He'll skin me alive. I hated breaking down in front of Tyb—until now I had done a pretty decent job of keeping things together. Now was the time that the past 48 hours had finally caught up with me.

Tyb said nothing, just stripped off his gloves, stepped forward, and wrapped his muscular arms around me. Such sweet, exquisite torture, to be in the embrace of a man I found indelibly attractive and dear God, lusted for. He smelled of soap and sweat, of earth and manly musk. I could feel his hand stroking my back in a soothing manner. A few moments of sobbing against his shoulder, I raised my face to his to apologize for getting his shirt wet with tears.

Instead, his lips met mine. Electricity surged through me, and I leaned into him more, cursing my clothing for impeding his touch against my skin. The gentle sensation of Tyb's tongue gliding across my lower lip had me silently begging for more of his kisses. Then, as sudden as it started, he stopped and I protested.

"I can't, Izzy. I can't." Tyb stepped away. "I want to, but I can't."

I tried to not take his words as rejection. "I'm sorry, Tyb." Now I felt like a dumbass.

"Christ, don't be!" The way he exclaimed that, made me think he felt the electricity, too. "But let's face it. I've been lonesome up here alone, I don't want to nail the first thing that catches my fancy just because I've been lonely. And honestly, I'm not into Marvin Gaye and *Sexual Healing*."

Well, why the hell not?

Chapter Fifteen

I felt embarrassed for melting into Tyb's arms the way I did. Embarrassed and mortified that I wanted more than he did. Or did he? Shit, anyhow, he defined his boundary. I tried to save face. "Yeah, I don't want to be another notch on a guy's bedpost."

With a smirk, Tyb turned around and began washing his hands at the tiny sink in the corner of the nearly-barren room. "You know, Izzy, I just never been the kind of guy to bang a chick just because he could. I enjoy the emotional aspect of intimacy as much as the physical, if not more. I was wrong to kiss you, and for that I apologize. It's the best way I know to make a woman stop weeping. You had every right to slap my face for being a fucking horndog. Next time, go for it."

"You don't need to apologize. Seriously. I'm embarrassed to mention it, but I married the only guy I ever kissed. I…I…I didn't know it'd feel so… good with someone I didn't know well. It's stupid. Forget I said anything." Pure mortification poured through every vein and artery in my body.

"Really? You never kissed another guy besides him?" Guess my admission was an ego stroke to him. His warm-sherry eyes burned bright.

It was my turn to blush. "Yes. I'm ashamed to admit such a horrid fact. Even sadder to say that the physical intimacy with him usually veered toward him-taking-things-out-on-me side. So my experience is very limited. So on that note, I think I extra-liked your kisses. But that's because I'm ig'nant, I guess." I cracked a half-smile. The way I figured it, if Christos is going to bring glittery nuclear zompires to life, then I might as well enjoy what time this earth has before King NutJob unleashes Armageddon upon us all.

"Since you made your confession, I'll make mine. I learned girls are trouble. Mara just threw some trouble my way, trouble with connections, *trouble* that is nearly irresistible. I'm only a man, Izzy. When there are things I want, I take them or make them. I don't have attractive women falling into my lap, as a rule. Let alone a woman running from her ex-husband, a very unstable ex-husband who already hates my guts, at that."

"Circumstances being what they are, it seems only natural to me. Adam and Eve in your Eden here." I could feel that I had nothing to fear from Tyb. Didn't need to watch my words or hide how I felt lest he get mad. I would take the bull by the horns with him. "If I'm starting my life over, then it's a complete do-over. I'm attracted to you Tyb. Was before you kissed me, and the lip lock didn't exactly make that attraction dull. I'm going to be stranded up here for a long time, so as I see it, we either get over this mutual attraction or we give into it and enjoy what time we have before shit hits the fan."

I watched him swallow slowly, his adam's apple bobbing while the look in Tyb's eyes seemed a cloud of passion and confusion. Or maybe it was me. Didn't know, didn't really care. Decided to go for the jugular. "Besides, Selesta is dead, you said so. So all her connections, all that *trouble*, doesn't apply to Izzy, now does it? You said so yourself."

Wish I could bottle that burning look in his eyes for lonesome winter nights. I felt on fire, and while a nice chunk of that was due to my audacity, the lion's share belonged to Tyb. "This could end badly. Then we're stuck up here with a person we detest."

"Maybe. Maybe not. But I will tell you some facts. I am not sexually aggressive—this is the first time ever I've been this sprung over someone. But you're right. I'll pretend not to be all into you and everything will be just fine, right?"

A moment that felt as long as years emerged in the silence between Tyb and I. Fuck it, he's not going to make me kick rocks, I knew that already.

"I'll think about it." That was all. Tyb whirled around and walked out one of the doors. I followed, pulling my jeans up. Oh My God. I just came onto a guy with my pants around my ankles and I didn't notice in heat of the moment. *Face, meet palm.*

"You'll think about it? Thank you for giving consideration to bumping uglies." We went down a short hallway, with three doors. He chose door number two. It led to a staircase. The staircase led to another hallway, again with three doors. "Where are we?"

"In the treehouse proper. And yes, I'll think about it." He stopped and turned to look at me, a puzzled expression on his face. "Why me?"

Dumbfounded, my mouth ran away with my tongue. "Why you? Because you aren't going to hit me, for starters. You're honest, and I appreciate that. Why am I throwing myself at you? Don't know, but to tell the truth, on my part, it doesn't feel too bad. Except for the awkward conversations like this, part. Otherwise, just because. I mean, you can teach me to whittle, and I guess I can carve myself a dildo—what grit sandpaper would I need to assure I wouldn't get any splinters *down there*?" I pointed as discretely to my nether region, relishing the crimson color infusing Tyb's face.

"You're going to be like this the whole time you're here?"

"Don't know yet. Do you want to find out?" I was more serious than not.

He swallowed again. "Not really. I'm not looking for strings, Izzy…"

"Me neither. Just got out of a relationship, you know. I don't want to put my head anywhere near something that can be used to tie me up." I winked. "I'm not a hussy, I swear."

"Never took you for one, Izzy." Tyb took a step toward me, reached out and tilted my chin up so he could look me in my eyes. The mournfulness emanating from his gaze took me aback. "I'm up for fun, but nothing more than that. Don't expect flowers from me, or poems. I'm not that kind of man. If you want sex, I can do that, but as a roommate with benefits sort of thing. And only when we both agree. You have your room, I have mine. Are you on birth control?"

"I have a couple packs of pills." Christos insisted I always travel with back up packs of pills, so I had no excuse for missing a dose.

"Okay. I ask because it's a far hike for a pregnant woman

to get anywhere near the local hospital. Can't risk you getting pregnant."

I nodded my understanding. It'd be hell to be snowed in, pregnant, and nearing time of delivery. There'd be no one to deliver a baby but Tyb.

"You sure you want me?" Tyb asked, his voice quiet in silent hall.

I bit my lip and whispered, "More than anything. Can't get it off my mind."

He closed the distance between us, backed me up against the wall and began kissing the hell out of me. Every time his lips met mine, it felt as though electricity played pinball with my senses. Tyb's callused hands grazed my neck, jawline, cheek, with feather-light touches.

I didn't mean to moan into his mouth with shameless need, but I couldn't resist the pleasure. His hands moved from my face to my collar bone, and then to my breasts. Through my shirt, he cupped and molded me in his hands. I shivered in anticipation as his whisker-roughened face moved to nibble kisses on my neck and behind my ear. Tyb noticed my quivering under his touch.

"You want me to stop?"

"Stop and you'll have to teach me to whittle."

He smiled, reached for my hand and led me through a door. The room we were in had a bed and nothing else. Like the ones in the house, it was quilt covered. He led me through that door, to the bed side. Tyb sat down and stood me between his open knees. Slowly, ever so slowly, he unbuttoned my shirt from top to bottom and kissed each inch of revealed skin.

This sensuous slowness drove me mad. My hands went for his jean's fly, fumbling with the belt. "Don't Izzy."

"Why?" I hoped he wasn't a touch-me-not like Christos.

"Because it's been a long time since I've been with a woman. I want to draw this out as long as I can."

I felt slick desire pooling in my panties. "You know, I'm up for a quickie and then taking our time once we get it out of our systems."

"Oh, woman, what you'll do to me…"

I smiled and bent to kiss his lips for a moment before

stepping away to strip down to my birthday suit.

Tyb got naked quicker than I did. Then I made a discovery that shook my world. In my inexperience, I thought Christos inordinately well blessed beneath the belt. I was wrong. Deadly wrong. That's like putting a stack of dimes next to a soda can. I gasped when I saw the length and breadth of Tyb's rock hard cock.

"How do you keep that in your jeans?"

"By thinking of jumping into the creek during winter."

"Is it going to fit?"

"Yes, but you're in the lead. I don't want to hurt you."

Now naked, I took the seat Tyb provided on his lap. He sat reclined on his elbows while I climbed atop, only to kneel and slowly sink onto his shaft. Couldn't believe the tumescent cock *not* tearing me asunder. Once I had him fully encased within, I began rocking back and forth, grinding hard on him. Tyb's hands held onto my hips, while I leaned over him, my hands next to his head. His lips parted and eyes half closed, I couldn't resist. Bent down and kissed him. His grip tightened and he began to move my hips back and forth, with ever-increasing ferocity. I broke the kiss and moaned.

"Oh God, Oh God, Oh God…"

"Don't hold back, Izzy. Don't hold back."

I couldn't hold back if my life depended on it. I was to the point of no return, the point where the slightest movement would send me spiraling into the land of satisfaction. Then I could feel it… feel Tyb, pulsating hard within me. He gave tiny thrusts until the pulsating took us both over the edge. The more he came, the harder the thrust, and the more frenzied I fucked him back.

Best orgasm ever. Covered in sweat, I collapsed on Tyb's chest. He put an arm around me, and it felt good. Fuzzy contentment reigned before I got my second wind.

Tyb had his eyes shut, when I spoke in a whisper in between kisses on his chest.

"Okay. I'm ready for round two."

Chapter Sixteen

"Izzy, we have things to do."

Why yes, that is why I'm naked right now, lying between Tyb's spread legs. *Things. To. Do.* Like Tyb, although he's not a thing. But the huge one-eyed monster standing at attention, well, that just begged for consideration. "I want to *do you*."

"You did me. Now we have to milk the goats before it gets dark." Amusement lurked in Tyb's husky voice.

"I did you, so now it's your turn to do me. I believe in equality of the sexes." My audacious statement had Tyb laughing.

"Here's what I propose. We do our chores, fortify ourselves with sustenance, and then hunker down in the house for the night. This treehouse is great and all, but the atmosphere is lacking."

Grey concrete walls devoid of windows reinforced Tyb's truth of our surroundings. "Okay. Then let's get going. I'm horny."

He laughed hard. Then again, so did I. Tried not to think what would happen when my stash of pills runs out. I can guarantee me having protection against pregnancy for now being the deciding factor of Tyb giving me some dickin'. Oh, what dickin' it was, too.

We dressed and Tyb showed me the way out of the treehouse that doesn't involve timers and self-shutting doors. A one-way door that will let people leave but won't let them in. It melded against the treehouse exterior, blending in so one wouldn't even notice. We walked back to the Mule, piled in, and headed off toward the goats.

I enjoyed traveling by Mule. Got to see more of the

landscape with forested hills and verdant meadows. A small creek snaked by the foot of some hillocks, cutting a swathe through the open spaces where grain grew and ripened beneath the sun.

Brad and Janet greeted us, tails wagging. "Time to milk, go bring 'em in." Tyb spoke to the shepherds, who in turn, bounded off to flank the spread-out herd of goats and urge them toward the milking shed.

Tyb opened the Dutch door, gathered his supplies and gave me a rundown of the milking procedure.

"First off, wash your hands and the goat's teat with this," he held up a package of antibacterial wipes. "You'll want to milk a squirt or two into the wipe, to clear out the nipple for milking. This stuff," this time, it was a spray can, "goes on after you milk. Helps keep bacteria out of the nipple because it takes about half an hour for it to close. Now, the goats sometimes won't stand still. If they step in the pail, that milk has to get chucked. Just toss it on the hill. It's a good fertilizer."

One by one, each of the goats got milked. For every one goat I did, Tyb did two. So, it went pretty fast and after I got over the initial embarrassment of grabbing another female's nipples in a quest for dairy goods, I got into the groove. Just didn't want to picture myself standing at a stanchion, head locked into place, munching peacefully at a bucket of oats while someone kept squeezing my boobs and playing with my nipples. Just don't think I had the fortitude. That says something about a goat, you know. They are freaks.

Tyb lead me, buckets in hands, to the spring box—a building with a stone trough running on the inside of three walls. In the trough were cans, tall with narrow openings. Also inside the trough, fast flowing water. "We have to cool the milk as soon as we can. Prevents bacterial growth. The only bacteria we want are the ones associated with cheese."

"What types of cheese do you make?"

"Want to see?"

"Yes. Oh, God yes."

Tyb quirked an eyebrow. "A fan of fromage?"

"Big time."

He nodded, finished filtering and pouring the milk into one of the tall cans and telling me about the wonders of spring boxes. "My stream flow rate is about fifteen gallons a minute— not bad at all. So, I diverted a part of the stream to feed the trough. It exits and heads toward the meadow for irrigation."

That chore done, Tyb led me back up toward the house. About ten yards from the house-hill, stood a building made of stones. No more than ten by eight, the way it fit into the natural landscape had its roof nearly level with the ground, with a rock staircase leading down into the chamber d' fromage.

After opening the heavy wooden door, Tyb stood to the side and gestured for me to walk inside. A wonderland of cheese! Shelves lined with wheels of cheese covered the walls. He gave me the tour of his culinary achievement. "I made some cheddar, feta, camembert, got a pretty decent blue in the spirit of Roquefort, been trying to master manchengo."

"Is there anything you don't know how to do?"

"Yeah. Put me in a suit and drop me in the city, I'm pretty sure I'd get lost."

Although I tried not to venture down that mental alley, I couldn't help resist comparing Tyb to Christos. While Tyb may think he'd be lost in the city, I'm pretty sure he'd find a way to escape to his hills before the sun had set. Christos… I don't think he could find his way from the hills and into the city within a week without a cellphone and credit card. The only thing I really didn't get about Tyb was how he survived so long devoid of socialization. Seventeen years is a long time.

"I'm heading up the house for a shower." I felt grimy and the incision on my butt was starting to ache now the anesthetic completely wore off.

"Okay. You can take your shower and I'll start dinner. You can finish dinner while I'm showering. Sound fair?"

"It does. Although I'm not much of a cook. Just a heads up on that." He began to walk with me up to the house.

Tyb sighed. "I mean no offense whatsoever when I ask, did you have any life skills outside the work place?"

"Define life skill." Yes, there was an edge in my voice.

"How did you survive?" That wasn't a definition, but I

understood what he was trying to grasp.

"I got married right out of college. Lesson learned, okay? I didn't have to do anything because anytime I did do something it meant I wasn't being dependent upon my husband like a good little subservient wife. I grew up in a small town, my friends weren't the farmer's kids. All I really needed to know was my clothes size and then, what topics not to mention within Christos' earshot lest I push him over the edge."

"So you were waited on hand and foot?"

"Pretty much. Really started resenting how I couldn't go anywhere without a chaperone, which went hand in hand with being in a gilded cage."

"I don't envy your past life."

"Me either." In reflection, it was empty. Christos wanted to domineer it, conquer and command it, leave no room for anything else.

An awkward silence crept forth to engulf us both. We made it to the front door and I opened it before Tyb had a chance to act the gentleman. We went inside and like clockwork, Tyb made for the kitchen sink to wash his hands. Again, I wandered to the bathroom and got the shower going. While it heated up, I got into my stash of Lush goodies and whipped out some Karma soap. Spiced orange and patchouli, without out fail, makes me feel like sunshine.

I took my hot shower after checking the bandage on my butt. Hardly any blood on it, just a thin line about half an inch long. Being that there was little blood, made me feel better about washing. While the soap's perfume besieged my senses, I thought about the quickie with Tyb.

Oh My God. I never thought I could orgasm so easily with very little stimulation, but the affect he has on me resulted just in that. He was tender, gentle. Looked down, and didn't see any new bruises. Amazing. It wouldn't be hard to get spoiled by Tyb's attentions.

Wrapped up my shower and headed to my room, clad in nothing more than a towel. Tyb's back was to me. Good thing too, otherwise the urge to flash him would have taken over.

I dressed in cut offs and a camisole, no bra. Time for

comfy. Left my room and made a beeline for the kitchen. Tyb stood at the stove, frying bacon.

"Sous chef, reporting."

Tyb turned and smiled. "Just in time. Fry the bacon. Then take the bacon out, and sauté the onions there," he pointed at the cutting board and about half an onion's worth of chopped up, eye-watering-flavor country. "When those are done, just chuck 'em in that salad bowl. Spinach salad tonight, with pork chops, apple sauce and baked taters."

Perhaps it's the mountain air that made me a ravenous beast. I did what was requested of me, had it done before Tyb was out of the shower. So I set the table. As I placed the glasses, Tyb came out of the bathroom. He wore plaid pajama pants that rode low on his hips, highlighting the bones and musculature that made Tyb into a statue of sinew. He didn't need to work out— homestead was enough exercise for him to be sculpted into an art form. As he exited the lavatory, Tyb put on a white tee shirt, hiding his six pack.

For a moment there, I wanted to pull a Janet Wiess and sing out, "I'm a muscle fa-an!" in protest of those abs being hidden away.

He strode over to me, his bare feet making slap-slap sounds on the hardwood floor. "How's dinner coming?"

"You tell me, *capitan*."

So, he did, proclaiming it done. Longest dinner ever, with the knowledge that round two still loomed. We ate in silence, cleaned up in silence. Then Tyb asked, "Want to watch a movie?"

"What do you have in mind?" Porn? That'd be a nice ice breaker.

"What sort of flicks do you like?"

"Musicals."

He quirked an eyebrow. "Musicals that involve corsets?"

"Yes. Heels and thigh-highs, too. And Tim Curry." And so I smirked.

"So, that rules out *FernGully, Muppet Treasure Island,* and *Annie*. Rocky for the win."

"There's just something about a man in heels who knows how to rock 'em…"

"So, into Tranny porn?"

"Uh, not really. Just Tim Curry porn."

So, we went to his room and turned the oversized computer monitor toward the bed. He cued up Rocky Horror Picture Show and we sat on his behemoth of a bedstead, resting against flannel-covered pillows. It felt a little odd, being so near to a virile man who wasn't Christos. Barely knew him, but what I did know of, I liked. A lot. Calm, logical, sexy, capable, intelligent, whimsical, kind… A world of color compared to the monotone shade of Christos.

"Why the sigh, Rocky not doing it for you?"

"He's still a sweet transvestite, but just got a lot on my mind. Last 24 hours finally catching up with me."

"It's been an interesting 24 hours."

"Yes, it has. Think I'm kinda in shock."

"It's possible. You okay, though?"

I liked that he asked. Maybe he just wanted to prep for possible waterworks. Maybe he actually gave a shit. Don't know, won't presume to know. "Yeah. Just trying to settle into the new me. Izzy. Don't even have a last name. Don't have a history. I'm me but not me. Can be anyone I want, I suppose. It's a new journey to find myself."

"Journeys are good for the soul. A decent journey will help shift your perspective in some matter, most likely totally unrelated to the reason for the journey." Tyb obviously learned that lesson firsthand.

I turned to face Tyb. "You know what would make Izzy feel like Izzy?" Because Selesta would *never* get away with such a thing?

"What is that?" Humor lurked in his eyes, warm and inviting like melted chocolate.

I didn't speak. Why break the silence with needless words when actions can convey so much more? I crawled onto his lap so that my legs were wrapped around him. "This." With excitement on my breath, I leaned in and kissed him. For a moment, his lips softened beneath mine, before firming up and taking the initiative. That's when I realized he held back earlier.

The passion flowing from his lips and into my being

fueled a fire between my thighs. Whisker-roughened skin rubbed against my cheek and Tyb whispered, "You're going to kill me before you embark on your new life, aren't you?"

Three quick kisses along his jawline to his ear, then I replied, silky-soft, "I hope not. It'd be a terrible way to repay your kindness."

"I don't want you repaying in sex."

"I'm not paying you with sex. I'm your farm minion now. The sex is my idea because I'm insatiably lustful where you are concerned. This voodoo that you do is some potent stuff." Tyb's hands reached around to grab my ass. He was mindful of my incision, too.

"Don't hold back tonight. I want to see you full throttle."

"You might not like me full throttle."

He laughed. As in, Tyb threw back his head and guffawed. "I don't know where you get that idea. I've been celibate as a monk for years. If you want to fuck my brains out, I say go for it. Tell me what you want and I'll make it so."

"Fine. Get naked and spank my ass." Wish I had a camera to capture the bemused expression that made its appearance. So on that note, I vacated Tyb's lap and made for the foot of the bed. Facing him, I stripped out of my clothes, and then knelt on the bedside, my ass in the air and my head cradled on my arms.

Didn't have to tell him twice. He dropped his pants and came to my side. Even flaccid, his cock's length was impressive. "What kind of spanking do you want? Hard or teasing?"

I'm glad he knows there's a difference. "Your choice. Just spank me. See how wet you get me."

Gauntlet thrown. Tyb began to smooth his calloused hands over my ass, caressing and kneading. Felt good. Then w*ham!* He smacked me in such a way that the heel of his palm hit my ass while his palm and fingers slapped against my sex. Sent tingles from my nethers to my brain almost instantly. Then he caressed my ass again. Then another well-aimed spank. "Any other kinks you have, Izzy?"

"A couple, in moderation. How about you?"

"I have one or two… Don't want you running for the valley, though."

"That shocking? You and your goats don't have a thing, do you?" I teased.

That delicious hand stopped its magic. "No. As lonely as I've been, I've never found *any* critter attractive. Here, hold on a moment."

His hand left my arse and it felt cold, devoid of his heat. He walked over to his dresser and picked up a framed photograph and brought it to me. Tyb handed it to me so I could study it. Old photo, could tell by the cars in the background and the hair styles of the three people. Two teenaged girls, dressed up as Magenta and Columbia from *Rocky Horror Picture Show*, and a teenaged boy, dressed as Frank N. Furter. "You rocked that corset."

"Indeed. That was the Halloween before I ran. I love corsets and heels."

I looked up to him; I'm sure the eagerness radiating from my eyes like lasers through smoke—very evident. "Would you?"

He smiled at me, hesitantly. "You sure?"

"I see no reason for you not to do so." I arose from my position. "If you don't want to, I understand. But I have no problem with it. I made my position on the subject known earlier." The thought of getting spanked by a man dressed up as a sweet transvestite… secret dream come true. Christos would never sport such stuff. An affront to his manliness which could only be fixed by beating something brunette and female.

"Sure, give me a couple minutes." Tyb took the photo from my hands and returned it to the dresser. Then his attention shifted to taking an armful of stuff from the bottom drawer to the bathroom.

I watched Rocky Horror. It was the part when Janet was singing *Toucha Toucha Touch Me* when Tyb reappeared, looking very much a young Tim Curry without the makeup.

"You're hot." And I felt like a nimrod for voicing my admiration, but the man has a great figure and quite frankly, his garb displayed it deliciously. The bonus was that he knew how to walk in heels with the same attitude as a runway model. I got in spanking position again, and without missing a beat, Tyb placed five spanks to the center of my lust. This time though, instead of caressing my ass, he slid a finger down my slit, sliding in my liquid passion.

I backed up against his hand, eager for him to pillage my depths. Instead, Tyb kept his touch non-committal and me, ever wanting his attention.

"So, besides spankings, what do you like?"

"Mmmmm… I like blindfolds. Sometimes being tied up—if it doesn't result in bruises or torture."

"Would you let me tie you up?"

I thought about it for a moment. "Only if I get a chance to tie you up as well, sometime down the line."

He contemplated and replied, "Sounds fair." His hands went back to massaging my bottom.

I wiggled my ass to remind Tyb of his duty. "I want you to fuck me."

"You do? I wouldn't have guessed."

"Do you want me to beg?"

"Do you want to beg?"

"No. I just want your cock in me."

Tyb removed his hands from me and asked me to lie on his bed. I did so, interested in where he was going with this adventure. "Close your eyes."

I did so, feeling his weight travel across the bed toward me. Then I could feel his hot breath panting over me. First at my feet, then up to my knees My thighs and their apex. Navel, torso, breasts and neck. Then my lips. I opened them, just a little, hoping he'd take the bait and kiss me. He didn't though.

Instead, he straddled my upper thighs. His hands fluttered from my belly, upward, to my breasts. Light as butterfly wings, he grazed my nipples with his fingers, then back down to my belly. Again and again, each pass became firmer. Then he flicked my taunt nipple with his fingers. Didn't hurt, just startled me a little. I let a low moan pass between my lips and writhed my hips beneath him. "I want more, Tyb."

As a reply, he began kissing my neck. Little teasing nips and licks made every hair stand on end. He worked his magical lips down to my collar bone, breasts, belly and pussy. He spread my thighs and began to lick and suck. I fucked against his face, but right before I peaked, he stopped and kissed me. I could taste myself on his lips and oh! It was a potent aphrodisiac. He pushed the tip of his tongue through my lips and I moaned in delight.

Tyb stopped for a moment and said "Open your eyes." I did so, watching him remove his bikini underwear.

I got up and moved to the bed's edge before he climbed back in. I lay on my belly and grabbed his cock, intent on sucking upon him. I wanted to taste the salty flavor of his excitement. My hand barely fit around the shaft as I licked the tip.

"No more, Izzy."

I sucked extra hard on the tip before letting go and scooting back into the center of the bed. Tyb spoke again, "No. On your knees, like earlier."

"As you wish." Flashed a smile in his direction before doing as he asked.

I knelt again, with my ass in the air, begging for Tyb's attention. His hands began caressing again. "You have a beautiful ass." *Whack!* I let out an excited peep. Didn't expect another spanking, was hoping for cock. "How do you want me?" *Whack!*

"Inside me!" Thought that was evident.

He slid another taunting finger down my slit and this time inserted two digits. Slowly, he moved them back and forth, then adding a third. I was slick and bucked against that hand.

"You want me?"

I was nearing another peak. "Yes, I want you. Fuck me, dammit!"

He laughed. "As you wish. Turn back over, please."

I did. I spread my legs so that I could lock them around Tyb and keep him close. He pulled me closer to him, so my ass almost hung off the bed. Then he had that magic wand of his in hand, rubbing his tip against my clit in delightful torment. Finally, he put his tip in me and inched his way forward, backing out a little before pushing further into my heat. I wrapped around him like a tight glove, squeezing his cock in excitement. Tyb held my legs up and began to thrust in earnest, the denial of such sweetness finally overwhelming him until he couldn't resist groaning with beast like intensity before bending over me, driving harder and deeper. My back arched and tried to bring him into me more, but it couldn't take him all. I felt stretched beyond impossibility and loving every moment. My arms reached around Tyb, holding him closer. Tried not to dig my nails into his back, but I couldn't resist giving into the ultimate pleasure he bestowed upon me. He wrapped one arm around me, supporting my neck and shoulders, while his other hand meandered from my thigh to my ass with every stroke of his cock. His lips plundered mine until I began clenching him tight inside me as I came with a ferocity I never knew I possessed.

"Oh God, Tyb… Keep fucking me hard, oh God yes!"

And he did so, finally burying himself nut-deep in me. Could feel his heat entering me as he came. For a moment, he lay in my embrace, then rolled off me to lay on his back.

"I'm pretty sure that if we keep this up, we're going to not last the winter."

"Why is that?" I asked, curious.

"You're a goddamn tigress, Izzy. You're going to wear me out."

"This is your second time in how many years you got some action and you think I'm wearing you out already? Hate to tell you Tyb, you have no idea how hot I find you and now that I know you're into corsets… well, I think I might be able to make up for your lost time."

He sighed deeply. "Well, if you don't kill me by then, I know I can count on your husband to do so."

I sat up and with my hand, tilted Tyb's face toward mine. His eyes, somewhat impassive, but with a trace of humor lurking in the dark. "I have no husband. I'm as single as you and just as eager to not get near a matrimonial noose. But I like this," I gestured from me to him, "we have good chemistry. And you fuck really well." I smiled. "Ready for round three?"

Tyb chucked. "Oh, yeah. You're going to kill me first. Death by kindness has to be the best way to go."

Chapter Seventeen

I climbed off Tyb's lap and lay next to him when his phone rang. He reached over me to fetch it from the nightstand.

He glanced down at the screen and smiled. "Want to see something funny? Try not to laugh."

I smiled, eager for this new adventure of his.

"Hey Mara… I need you to hit Costco before you head up here… yeah… okay, I need you to pick the biggest box of condoms they have. Must be Magnum Size."

My jaw dropped. Oh my. So, he has a back-up plan for when my pill supply runs out. Evidently, Mara's jaw dropped too, but she got collected faster than I. Could hear her yelling at him. Screaming. Cursing the skies that bore witness to his existence, even. She was *pissed*.

"You fucking fucked her? How could you fucking do that? You want to die, little man? I will fucking scorch the earth if you cost me Aisha, you motherfucker. Oh, wait, she never had kids. You're a fucker, Tyb, a goddamn fucker!"

"Calm down, Mara. It's not like that..." She stopped with the bellowing and now I could only hear his side of the conversation. "It's cool, sis. Just take it down a notch, okay? What?... No joke? What does the intel say? Can we move in? … Shit. That long? So what do we do until then? …. Okay. As you say, Mara. Gonna send you a text with some instructions. You have the connections to make it happen…. Okay, thanks. Much appreciated. But I'm serious. Get a lot of condoms if it's going to be that long. I'm going to need them." He hung up with a bemused expression. "She's good at dropping bombshells. She found Aisha." Before setting his cell phone down, he whipped out the text to his sister.

"Her twin? Where is she?"

Tyb turned to me and asked, "What do you know of Isle of

Twilight?"

"Never heard of it."

"It's an island your husband owns. Has a laboratory of his. Aisha is there."

My jaw dropped. Christos owns an island and never told me about it? Shows how much he trusted me. That, and he had to tag me like a wild beast to keep tabs.

"Can she be freed?"

"In theory, but it'll take years of maneuvering. It's not a tropical island. It's in the Arctic Circle. The Russians tested the world's largest nuclear bomb near there. Security is tight."

"So we wait until preps have been made?"

"Pretty much." He sounded dejected.

"Hey, at least you know where she is, right? That's a huge improvement over not knowing where. Will you tell your parents?"

"No. They disowned Aisha when she began subbing for Haytham. They did their research on him, decided that if Aisha wasn't good enough to date, she wasn't good enough to play with. Little sis didn't agree. It's my fault, though. Her running off with him."

"How could it be your fault? You were up here. Can't picture you telling her to run into his abusive arms."

"Aisha has always been special. She's gifted artistically. She's temperamental, always has been. She and Mara are alike but completely different. I was the only one in the family who could talk Aisha down and then I disappeared. She'd come up during the summers and help me build this house, but then she ran right into the arms of the fucker who ran me off the road, when she turned eighteen." Bitterness ate at Tyb, filled his voice with a mixture of admiration for his sister and hatred for Christos.

"You don't know that you disappearing is directly to blame. You aren't responsible for any one's actions other than your own."

"That may be, but family is *family*."

"What if Aisha doesn't want to come back?"

Tyb looked taken aback at such a thought. "Why would she want to stay?"

I shrugged my shoulders. "I don't know. I'm just throwing that out as a thought."

"She'll come home." Total conviction echoed in Tyb's expression.

"So when will Mara be up?"

"She'll be a day early. Day after tomorrow."

"I can't believe you asked her to buy condoms."

"Well, when she sees the reality of the situation, she'll agree with me. She doesn't like it though. My involvement with you jeopardizes, in her view at least, the ability to taunt Haytham with you. She'd love to use you as bait."

Okay, wow. Did not like the thought of Zamara using me as bait to get Christos. I can totally understand her reasoning, but yeah, don't like it. "Use me as bait?" Please let that mean visual, not a hostage exchange sort of situation.

"You'll make him see red, lose reason. I've got no doubt that dropping your name would result in some sort of action by Haytham."

"I don't like that at all. I don't want to be near him again." I began to hyperventilate. No, no, no, no! Never again to be subjected to Christos Haytham's whims. I'd rather die first.

"You won't. Mara's tirade gave me an idea. Revenge of sorts, for both of us."

I could feel my eyebrows lift. "Revenge?" Curiosity killed this cat.

"What would drive Haytham crazy?"

"Knowing I'm alive." Duh.

"No. Knowing you are alive and happy and getting fucked royally by another guy."

Whoa. "That wouldn't drive him crazy. That'd incite him to spree killing." My heart beat faster than Thumper's hind legs.

"He won't kill you."

"How do you know?"

"I'll kill him first. For Aisha and you."

"You don't owe me anything, Tyb. Giving me a place to hide and a cock to ride is more than enough. I don't know how I can even begin to repay you since farm work seems so insignificant in the scope of what I owe."

"Izzy darlin', you aren't the first person I've hidden from the big, bad, world. You owe me nothing. I don't ever want you to think of paying me back. There is no price for a person's life."

"I have another confession, Tyb."

"Should I put on the garb of a friar?"

"Only if you'll fuck me if I'm dressed as a nun."

"You have a delightfully twisted mind, Izzy." He smiled bright. "I like you."

I smiled. "That was my confession. I like you, too." More than I should, at any rate. Although my courtship with Christos was a whirlwind of commanding and bribing, it didn't have this natural feel that my time with Tyb—short as it's been, has seemed to possess.

I needed to make plans for when I get to reintegrate with society. I mean, if the world didn't end before that. Did I want to go back to Washington? Move back home, to Oregon? *Or stay in the mountains of California, hidden away from the worries of the world in this self-sufficient paradise?* I didn't mean for that thought to take hold, but it seemed so appealing. Maybe my opinion would change with the seasons, perhaps winter is the Big Suck up here (and not in the fun way)… Maybe Tyb will be over getting laid to his heart's content and not want me around. I can't invite myself. But the thought of Tyb offering me to stay when this is all over… Would I accept? Could I accept? No matter what, I'm jumping the gun at this point.

But the niggling thought that in the past 24 hours with Tyb have felt more secure, relaxed and laid back than the two years with Christos. That's an epic revelation. How could I ever believe Christos my soul mate? How could I have been that delusional? To be treated with honest respect from a guy was such a shocker. My opinion mattered to Tyb.

Dammit, he needs to be not so likeable. Or lickable.

Chapter Eighteen

A voice screaming, "TYB!" woke me up from the best sleep I have had in years. I bolted upright, clutching the quilt to my chin before recovering. Could hear Tyb's bedroom door open and his voice respond.

"Jesus, Zamara. Don't ever wake me up like that!"

I got up from my bed and wandered my door. The tone Zamara used could be likened to a Valkyrie war cry before gallons of blood is spilt. If the siblings were going to get into an argument, I'm going to stay out of their way. Zamara sat on the mass rocket heater's bench, while Tyb leaned a shotgun against the wall.

Mara was about to hand Tyb a large envelope when she spoke. "Got what you wanted. You sure about this?"

Tyb reached for it. "Yes. Absolutely certain."

She held it out of his reach. "Before I hand it over, I need to know… Did you have another dream?"

Tyb nodded. "Yes. The night before you called for me to take on this project."

Awe poured from Mara's expression. "You haven't had one of those for years."

"I know. Which is why this is important to me."

Mara clapped a hand to his shoulder and said, "I hope it works out. Your dreams aren't bullshit, but still… it's not logical." She handed him the envelope.

I walked out of my room. "Hallo, Zamara."

"Yeah, didn't mean to wake you up, Selesta. But he's on my shit-list."

"Don't be mad at him. I threw myself at Tyb. He told me

'No' a few times, too." I felt embarrassed to tell her that, but still, the blame is mine. I pushed the envelope.

"Saying no and following through are two different things."

"I didn't give him a choice, Mara. It was either give me what I want or help me whittle a dildo. He didn't like the idea of a sharp thing near a penis, evidently. He capitulated. I seduced him with bravado."

Mara looked from me to Tyb and back to me. "*You* said that?"

Tyb and I both nodded. "Yeah, I did. I'm not a hussy, I swear. But he brings it out in me."

Mara swiped a hand over her face in a tired gesture. "Goddamn your fucking dreams, Tyb. This makes things a little…Hmm, shaky, shall we say? You don't want to poke the pissed off grizzly bear with a sharp stick in its eye."

"Yeah I do. I want to blind him with that stick, first. He'll do something stupid if he's pushed. He'll lose sight of what he wants to get even. He's petty like that."

"Your little bower from him won't be so safe if he gets pissed enough. He'll raze the goddamn countryside on a quest for blood."

Tyb looked absolutely certain. "He can raze. He'll still end up at the wrong end of my pointy stick. I've got a couple advantages over him, the least being that I can be patient. Besides, he'll never know what will hit him. Is that postal box still available?"

"The one from years ago? Yeah. I still have the key and have been paying for it… Going to be placing an order soon?"

"Yup. Still buddies with the satellite guy?"

"Why yes I am. What's your plan, Tyb. I can see the hamster running on its wheel in your head. You're up to mischief."

"I'm toying with an idea, is all. I can guarantee it'll get a reaction from Haytham. I can guarantee he'll get enraged and I can guarantee that it'll bring him out of hiding."

"And what purpose does this fulfill?" Mara's expression seemed very unamused with Tyb.

"He'll come raging like a bull from where ever he is. Team A takes him down, Team B storms the castle and rescues Princess Aisha from the clutches of Haytham. You'll be on Team B, I know you'll like going Commando."

"Hey, the Commandos drink a lot of tea. They are a respectable lot."

I sat in silence, wondering just how exactly we'd bait Christos. "So, how exactly do we get him out of hiding? I know it'll involve me."

Tyb looked at me with his shrewd, amber eyes. "I'm trying to think of a way to piss him off royally without you being naked on the internet."

Well, okay then. "Me just being alive?"

"Not enough. We want 'Insane in the Membrane' kind of anger."

Mara broke the silence. "You know, her naked would just drive him nuts…"

"There are only two things that Jakob Haytham holds dear beyond belief. His power and his toys. He never liked competition. Wouldn't even have to be hardcore to piss him off. Just the thought of some other man between my thighs would set him off."

"I want you to think about planting that thought, Izzy." At Mara's bewildered expression, Tyb explained, "Selesta died over that cliff. She's Izzy."

"Well, that makes things convenient." Tyb's brow knit and Mara finished her thought. "When you open the envelope, you'll see."

"Okay, so no matter the method for pissing in Christos' eye, said urine needs to be delivered to his eye. How will this happen?"

Tyb spoke with a smirk. "I was thinking maybe we'd text him from an untraceable phone or email him through a series of proxy servers. Send him an URL. At the end of that, a message from Izzy, here, invoking the ghost of Selesta. Could taunt him into stupidity. He'd try to track where the image sourced from, but would either hit a brick wall or have to buy the company to get that info. The reason I suggested naked, is because porn is a multi-billion industry. He'd either go broke buying all the different sites we could use, because they won't go cheap, try hacking and get busted, because again, this is a multi-billion industry and they don't want people cashing in for free. Either way, that squeaky-clean image of his would be tarnished from the proximity of porn. Hey, Mara, what's the word about the explosion?"

Mara drew a deep breath. "They found a faulty containment block. Triggered a domino effect and the whole building fell. The isotopes used in his experiment weren't stable, and they unleashed what amounts to fallout from the vaporized building. Word has it that Haytham left the building exactly fifteen minutes before hell was unleashed. He's been laying low, although CIA believes he's holed up with some Russian mafia doofs up north. They aren't really subtle, but with the firepower they're packing, they don't have to be."

"And Aisha?" The hope Tyb had at news of his little sister shone through his voice like the sun breaking though a cloudy day.

"You won't like it. Either of you."

Don't know what Christos could do any more shocking than what's been mentioned already. "I feel dead where he's concerned, so don't hold back for my sake."

"Tell me, Mara."

She drew a calming breath and said low, "Aisha is with him. She's his assistant. They were caught on camera going over the Bay Bridge in the same car. Same at the airport, getting onto his private plane."

"WHAT?" Tyb bellowed, angered. "She's with him? What, was he cheating on hia wife?"

"He always cheated, Tyb. Doesn't matter the game, he'll pay o he'll be on top." My calm voice brought Tyb out of his anger.

"No bastard should do that, though. And I'm pissed that Aisha is with him. Glad she's alive, but still…"

"She won't come willingly. She loves him. That's not the worst part."

"What's the worst part?"

"He gave her a disease."

At Zamara's words, my mind flew as to whether I had that disease too, a by-product of Christos' unhealthy appetites. She looked to me and shook her head. "You're in the clear and I'll tell you why." To Tyb, she said, "I need to tell you about something science can do. It's called Virteria Serum and it's a fucked up nightmare our sister is infected with."

Chapter Nineteen

"I'm not sure I get it, Mara. Zombies? Vampires? People bombs?"

"If you can grasp that much, then you got it all, Tyb."

"And Aisha… she's one of them?"

"She's kind of between worlds. From what I found out, she has a first generation implant—as long as she has the implant, the urge to feed is quelled. Take out the implant, she gets a hankering for blood. She already is at the secondary stage of infection and that implant is the only thing holding her back."

"What's that about infection?" Tyb asked with no emotion in his voice. His eyes dulled with all that Mara told him.

"Her skin begins to crystallize and refract light. She looks like a raver covered in glitter. If she bites someone infected with the Virteria Serum, they'll both explode in the third stage."

"So he made Aisha into a weapon? He's going to kill her!" Tyb sat upright, rigid like a post, with tension binding him like a glue.

Mara's tone softened. "She asked for it, Tyb. She wanted to and signed a contract saying as much. His idea of assisted suicide."

He ran an impatient hand through his dark curls. "So….What? We don't get her away from him? Let that fucker just blow her up?"

Mara shrugged. "If we get her out of there, she'll raise hell just to get back to him. You know how she is. Giving up the ghost is something she can't do."

"So we do nothing, then?" Bitterness and anger directed at the situation echoed from Tyb's voice. "Sit on our asses and think happy thoughts?"

"I didn't say *that*. But we need to proceed carefully. If you want to provoke him, fine. But be aware, you could be provoking

Aisha as well."

"Well, that puts a damper on things, doesn't it?" Sarcasm: Tyb's sharpest sword.

"Just a little. Then again, it might be something he'll keep from her. She's not stable when she's upset. She's never been stable."

I piped up. "So what do we do? Just lay low or what?"

Mara nodded. "Pretty much the only choice." She addressed Tyb. "Look, if you want to fuck with Haytham, I can send you the gear to do so without getting busted." She dug into a small courier bag which seemed to serve as her purse and pulled out a key ring. In barely a moment, she freed a tiny brass key and handed it over to Tyb. "I'll send everything to the PO box. Just pick it up and use what you will." She then pulled a large duffel bag from off the ground onto her lap and opened it up. "Here. You wanted these, take them. And please, if you need more, just order them online and ship them to the box. I will never do *that* again for you, so don't ask. I hated getting smiled at by the cashier when he scanned them." Zamara threw a large box of condoms at Tyb. "One hundred fifty should last you two a while, right?" She held up a hand. "Wait. I don't want to hear the answer. Trust me." Then she stood up. "I'm going to crash in the treehouse. Still have cable TV patched through there?"

"Yeah. Remote is in the plastic tote."

"You and your totes." Mara readied her bags, slinging them over her shoulder.

"They serve a noble purpose. Don't bag on me for being prepared."

"Whatever, Tyb. I'm heading out before daybreak. Shit to do and whatnot."

"Thank you Zamara. For everything."

"Shut up, Tyb. Thank me when this is all over with, okay? Got a whetstone in a tote? I need to hone my KA-BAR."

"Yep. Look in the prep area, it'll be in a drawer."

Zamara grabbed her bags and walked out the front door, shutting it with a small slam.

"Is she always like a hurricane?" I asked. Clock said it was 2:30 in the morning. Who whirls into the middle of nowhere in the middle of the night? Only someone with a serious mission.

"She's mellowed out since she was younger. Not much though." Tyb stretched his arms above his head. I noticed stubble darkening his chin. "I'm tired but awake."

"Me too. Think I'm going to shove off to bed."

For a moment, a flicker of shyness darkened Tyb's face. "I, uh, was wondering if you wanted to uh, see something in my room."

I looked to the box of condoms on his lap, then back up to his face, quirking my brow with a silent question.

He laughed. "Actually, no." Tyb stood up and walked to his bedroom, grabbing the propped shotgun on his way. The envelope Zamara gave him was tucked under his arm, and the box of condoms in his other hand.

I followed, curious as to what he'd want to show me. When I entered his room, I saw him slide the shotgun under his bed. He stood up, put the box of condoms in his nightstand and then sat on his tousled bed. He held the envelope. I sat down next to him and asked, "What's that?"

Slowly, he opened the envelope and pulled out two bundles of paper-clipped documents. He handed me one. On top, a drivers license with a photo that looked a lot like me with shorter hair. Beneath that, a Social Security card and birth certificate. I flipped through the pile of papers and Tyb spoke.

"When it's safe for you to go, there's your ticket to your new life." There was a tinge of sadness to his voice. Wasn't sure if it was due to what he discovered about Aisha.

"I…I don't understand, Tyb."

"Fake ID and the whole lot—CIA issued. Everything you need to start over." He looked over and read the name saying, "Izabeau D'Beafort."

"Thank you, Tyb." Why though? Wasn't it a long time until I'll be in the free and clear? Then a thought hit me. Had to ask. "I overheard Mara ask you something about dreams. What kind of dreams?"

Tyb gathered my passport to freedom with a pensive look on his face. "I'm going to put this in the panic room for safety. If you need them, they'll be in the tote." As he slid them into the envelope, he said, "I have weird dreams. Like, screaming in the middle of the night. The dreams aren't scary or freaky, but I can't control myself from making the noise. They always strike before something in huge changes in my life."

"When was the first time you had one?"

"Two weeks before I got ran off the road. In my dream, I was putting a tent and duffel bag of supplies under a berry bush off the road a bit. Had that dream six nights straight. Ended up tooling down the road and finding that bush. The next day, I hauled out the tent and supplies, hid them, just like in the dream. What do you know? Like a week later, no more than twenty feet away from my wrecked car, was that berry bush with my stuff. Took it as a cue. I listen to those shitty dreams. They haven't steered me wrong, yet."

"That's like the second-sight." I was amazed. Didn't know stuff like that could really happen.

Tyb shrugged his shoulders. "I don't know. It is what it is."

"You told Zamara that you had one the night before she called you."

"Yeah, I did." His voice grew quiet.

"Can I ask what the dream was?"

He looked at me, with a mixture of dread and tiredness in his voice. "You don't want to know, Izzy. Suffice it to say it involved you coming into my life."

I looked at him, wanting to know what he wasn't telling me. "Did your dream tell you that you were going to get laid like crazy?"

He chuckled. "No, that was a pleasant surprise."

"There's more to it, isn't there?" Dammit, I want details.

"I don't want to lie to you, Izzy, but I don't want to corrupt things, either. Please don't ask questions I can't answer." He shook his head, as though it would reinforce his words.

"But you *can* answer. You chose not to, and leave me in the dark."

Tyb gave me half a smile. "I like you, Izzy. I don't know you much, but I know you have a good spirit. Maybe all these years alone have taken a toll on my mental state where women are concerned. Or not." The smile left his face, and I missed its sunshine. Even his eyes seemed to grow distant. "But I can't let you always have your way, not at this moment. Please accept that there are some things people aren't meant to know." His tone softened. "If I didn't think that you knowing would impact the future, I would tell you. After we deal with Haytham, if you're still interested, ask me again. You'll get a straight answer, I promise."

I nodded, content that he'd tell me. You know, if we survived shit hitting the fan and stuff. I stood up and leaned over quickly to brush a kiss to Tyb's cheek. "Goodnight." Not sure why, but he didn't seem to mind.

Blood flooded his face, and he smiled again. "Goodnight to you too."

I walked to the door and said, "If glittery zompires where going to attack us, and we only had minutes to live, would you tell me then?"

Tyb's eyebrows were jacked to the sky as a bemused smirk took hold on his lips. "Maybe. Guess we'll have to find out, eh?"

Chapter Twenty

Two days passed in relative quiet. I settled into my new schedule. Up before the sun, milk the goats, filter and cool the milk. Feed chickens, collect the eggs and avoid Gene Simmons, the rooster.

That fucking rooster.

"You named him after the KISS singer?" Could not hide my disbelief.

Tyb's arms were crossed over his chest as he leaned against a tree, waiting to see me scatter a mixture of seeds and grains for the chickens to attack. "Look at him, Izzy. He's black and silver with some red. Tell me he doesn't look like a member of KISS. He's the showman, the front man. That's why he's *Gene*."

I'll admit, the first couple days were weird. I felt like an intruder in Tyb's domain, although he never gave the impression that I wasn't welcome. It was just odd, this transition from continual walking on egg shells to being roommate to a guy who seemed pretty laid back. Since the incredible night of sex, he hasn't made a move toward me, nor I him. It was like we just needed to get that over and done with so we could move on.

As much as I wish it weren't so, my inexperience with men made it difficult to accurately judge what Tyb was thinking. Maybe he was just giving me space to adjust? Otherwise, there was little said between he and I other than random small talk. A part of me didn't mind. The other part of me disliked the silence. But I chalked that up to me used to Christos snapping on a regular basis. It was just… Weird.

The fourth night I tried cooking dinner. Can't go wrong with hamburgers, right?

Ha. Thank goodness for Mrs. Jones and her wonderful

cooking because my experience in the kitchen rivaled Christos' experience of being sane.

I pulled out a butcher's paper wrapped bundle of ground beef. Made two patties and started frying them in the cast iron pan that Tyb favored. Wasn't long before I had my nose above the pan, sniffing the meat. Something smelled off about my hamburgers.

Tyb walked from the bathroom, fresh from his shower, and over to me, witnessing my meat-huffing with some amusement. "What's up, Izzy? Having a problem?"

"I'm not sure. Something about this hamburger doesn't smell right."

He looked down into the pan. "That's not hamburger."

I stood upright and looked at him. "What was it? The ground up remains of a Haytham family member?"

He laughed. "No. That's wild boar Italian sausage."

"Oh. Well, shit. There goes cheeseburgers for dinner."

"Don't say that. We can make it work. Get the mozzarella from the fridge and slice it. I'm going to get some pasta sauce."

With a smirk, I asked, "Running to the store?"

"No, just the root cellar." With that, he bounded out of the kitchen and out the front door.

Couple minutes of serious sizzling atop the stove then I flipped my Italian burgers over just as Tyb came back into the house, jar of red sauce in hand.

When he reached my side, Tyb cracked open his sauce and took a whiff. "Mmmm. These will be kick ass burgers, Izzy. Wait and see."

"How's the sauce going to be used?" Condiment? Italian ketchup of sorts?

"We'll simmer those patties in the sauce. Pop the pan in the oven for a while, let the magic happen. We'll top with the mozzarella and have a salad, if that sounds good to you."

"Sounds better than plain hamburgers. Yay, teamwork."

"Yay, teamwork." He poured half the tomato sauce over the cooking meat and then gave the pan a good shake. "Can you turn the oven on to three-twenty-five?"

I did so, then went about the task of slicing the cheese.

After Tyb slid the cast iron pan into the oven and closed the door, he turned to me and began hesitantly speaking. "I... uh, just want to apologize for the other night."

What the hell was he talking about? "I'm puzzled. What exactly are you apologizing for?" All things considered, he's been non-offensive.

He licked his lip. "Not explaining my dream to you."

"You don't need to apologize, you didn't do anything wrong. It's your prerogative to keep things on a need to know basis. The worst offense I can accuse you of is making me curious as to how I play into your dream. Nothing more."

"Do you still want to know?" His deep gaze held me enthralled.

"Only if you'll tell me now since you brought it back up."

He sighed and replied, "I won't tell you the whole of it, but some. Is that acceptable?"

"Yes." How could it not be? Unless it made me wonder more, that is.

A moment of silence. "I dreamed that you'd be up here for a while."

"And the fake identification plays into that how?" Because curious minds want to know.

"They are for when you get sick of isolation and want to move onto new things in populated areas."

"You saw that I was going to high-tail it out of here?"

"Well, no, not exactly. But I'm a bit country and you're pretty rock and roll."

I looked Tyb straight in the eye and spoke in a deadpan voice, "I am not an Osmond."

"Technically, neither am I. But you know what I mean."

"No other reason other than me pining for the city life again?"

"We'll use them when we need them. But I don't see that happening anytime soon. Anyway, how's the incision?"

"It's not tender anymore." In fact, it healed pretty quickly.

"Good. So, we got about half an hour before dinner's done.

What do you want to do?"

A Cheshire cat smile formed on my lips. "I could tell you, or I could show you."

Lust glazed Tyb's chocolate eyes. "Show me."

My heart picked up its tempo as I smiled. With his back against the counter, I looked up into his gaze and leaned in to kiss him. After a moment, I broke away and whispered, "I have a request."

"So do I." His deep voice, husky with rising passion.

"Go first," I prompted, as curiosity washed over me.

"I'm horny, Izzy. I want you."

With a grin I replied, "Well, so happens I'm rather frisky for you, too. But my request is, uh, a little not vanilla."

He quirked an ebony eyebrow. "Do tell."

I bit my lip a moment before whispering, "Ravish me."

"Ravish you? Like a tawdry romance novel?" I deeply appreciated him not busting into laughter.

A giggle escaped my lips. "Very much so."

"May I be a little rough?"

"Yes. No bruises, though."

"Can I just propose no intentional bruising *ever*? That way it's never on the bargaining table. I'm not a beast, Izzy. Last thing I want to do is hurt or otherwise injure you. I don't feel the urge to brand you like a beast or a piece of property."

I felt the need to explain. "I don't mean to imply that you would deliberately mark me. No offense intended. And I agree, it's off the table. I just didn't want to assume, you know?"

"No offense taken. Let's set the boundaries for your definition of *ravishment*."

"Be rough, pin me down, tear my clothes off…"

"Dominate you?" The way he said it made my nethers tingle with anticipation of how he'd dominate me.

"Yes."

"Go hide. I'm going to set the timer for five minutes and wait in my room. When I come out, your ass is mine."

I smiled wide, pleased he liked my idea. "We can call this game the Viking and the Villager."

"One more kiss before we play." Tyb pulled me close and pressed his body against mine. His jeans outlined the bulge of his arousal. I ran an eager hand over his hardness while kissing his lips.

"I could get used to this," I whispered against his lips.

"Me too, Izzy."

"Wait before you set that timer. I want to change into something less utilitarian and more shred-happy."

Tyb nodded. "I'm going to my room to get in character. Set the timer when you're ready. If things get intense for you, what's your safe word?"

"Purple."

He smiled and moved to turn the oven down. Looked like it was in the mid-200's now. "This will buy us more time."

"The Vikings are a randy lot."

"This Viking is the randiest of them all. Will have to take a special Village lass to tame his permanently hard cock."

"Must be awkward, trapped on a long ship with nothing but men for company, and permanent erection."

Tyb laughed. "Hurry, before I set that timer to three minutes." He turned around and went to his bedroom. I went to mine.

Can't believe how aroused I get at the thought of playing with Tyb! The excitement could barely contain itself. How could I live without feeling this level of lust? I stripped out of my clothes and pondered my options. Couldn't come across a better one than my birthday suit.

Heh. Can't wait to see his face when he finds me.

Chapter Twenty-One

Right before I headed out my bedroom door, I changed my mind about the attire. I put on the oldest tee-shirt I had, which wasn't old at all. Christos never allowed me to keep anything faded or worn, no matter how much I liked the clothing. So, black tee-shirt and I put on blue cotton panties. I'm willing to sacrifice them on the Altar of Lust.

A shiver ran from my brain down my spine as I realized something. I didn't like Christos when he dominated me, because he used the opportunity to punish me, more often than not. I knew I could count on Tyb to be cool and in control of the situation. Then again, I don't fear Tyb. That makes a world of difference in what I'm willing to explore with him. Fear and sex is not a good combination. And fear was a mainstay of my relationship with Christos.

After I left the room, I made my way to the kitchen, and then stopped as inspiration struck. Four pillar candles of various sizes waited on the counter top. I lit them and left them in strategic areas: one on the counter, one on the rocket mass heater, one in the bathroom and the last on the coffee table by the couch, near Tyb's bedroom door. Went back to the stove and set the timer for four minutes, with a smirk on my face. Then I turned off the lights. I knew where I was going to hide. I took a handful of walnuts from the bowl on the table and made for my spot.

I walked as quietly as I could for the atrium. Little stone pathways divided the garden beds, and I hid behind the tallest bush residing in the greenhouse. It lived in a corner, and now, I pressed myself into that dark nook and waited.

Seconds seemed as long as minutes, and each minute eking by, felt like a year. The golden light from the candles didn't quite make it all the way to me, but that's okay. While I waited, I tried to get comfortable. The vaguely lemon scent of the bush's foliage tickled my nose. Tiny oval leaves brushed against my skin, eliciting a body-wide tingle of anticipation. What kind of Viking would be he? The Fabio-esque Catherine Coulter special? Or the rapacious kind? Byzantine guard? Slaver? So many roles he could play. So many roles to explore.

Then like a gunshot, the timer went off, filling the house with an irritating *buzzzzzz* I could hear Tyb's bedroom door open and his hurried footsteps *slap-slapping* across the floor. Then the buzzer silenced. My heart beat fast, adrenaline pumped through my body as I eagerly awaited Tyb's move.

His feet gave a vague idea of where he was at any given time. But Tyb the Viking didn't seem to hell-bent on conquest quite yet. He seemed more interested in getting a glass of water.

Finally, he left the kitchen and sounded like he meandered to the couch. Then finally, the role of pillaging Viking seemed to take hold. He let out a guttural growl which sent tingles flying across my skin. I never did role play like this, and it excited me to no end.

His pace changed. Now his footfalls were heavy with intent. He paced around the living space, and I could hear things being moved, like the couch and kitchen chairs. Then his footsteps came my way. I smiled, and readied a walnut. As soon as Tyb crossed over into the atrium, I gently chucked a walnut low to the ground, into the living room. It rolled with a clatter and the Viking turned around and pounced. I stifled a giggle.

I aimed another walnut for a dark corner and threw. I could see Tyb through the foliage hiding me when he made his way for that corner with even more intent. Was just about to lob another one when by candlelight, I saw him pick up a walnut. Oops. Found out already. He stood tall and looked around. I assumed he was looking for a line of sight. He turned until he looked my way. I licked my lips and smiled. I knew he couldn't see me in the dark. I also knew I have two more walnuts. With darkness as my ally, I tossed one into the garden bed opposite of me, on the left-hand side of the atrium. Tyb quickened his step and made a bee-line for the atrium. Oh, the look on his face excited me, and that liquid excitement centered itself in my pussy.

Candlelight works magic upon people, and his face was half-silhouetted against the black. Tyb's forehead, thick lashes and the angle of his cheek, flowing into that square jaw, all highlighted by golden light.

Then I noticed he was completely nude and already erect.

I threw the last walnut as hard as I could into the corner furthest from me. With his back turned, I darted from my spot to find somewhere to hide anew.

Tyb heard me burst through the greenery and lunged for me. With a squeal of delight, I evaded his grasp and ran for the living room. The couch now blocked my bedroom and the bathroom door. I jumped over the back and made for the bathroom, so happy it was an inward-swinging door. I locked it. Barely a breath later and then pounding at the portal.

"Go away, heathen! You shall not take my gold or burn my church!" Oh, I was getting into the spirit of this.

"If you open the city gates, I will not steal your gold nor torch your sacred places. I want one thing and one thing only!"

"What is this one thing, and if you get it, will you go away and leave the city in peace?"

"I demand one comely wench for the night. If she can appease my appetite, then I will let your people live in peace. I vow this, and may Thor strike me now and repeatedly if I lie."

"The Elders will discuss your terms. The Elders accept your terms."

"Then send out the wench!"

I opened the door and put my hands behind my back. I looked down at the ground. "The Elders have sent me to be the Viking sacrifice."

Tyb grabbed the back of the couch and pushed hard, moving it from the door and allowing him entry. He picked me up like I weighed nothing and heaved me over his shoulder, his hand caressing my ass. Then he put me on the ground.

"Are you afeared of me, wench?"

"Yes. You are a rapacious Viking!"

His hand touched my face. "Look at me."

I raised my eyes to his burning gaze.

"I see your Elders chose well. They must love their gold."

He grabbed my shirt by the collar and tore it. Cool air hit my skin and it prickled with eagerness. Tyb's rough hand smoothed its way from my waist to my breast, weighing it in his hand. "If you please me well, I may let you live, wench."

I chose that moment to move from his hold and run for the kitchen. He caught me made two steps for freedom. With an arm around my waist and another pinioning my hands together, I struggled and tried to be dead weight to him. Didn't work. He was too strong.

His hand moved from my waist and back to my breast, plucking the nipple before rolling it between his forefinger and thumb. Then he picked me up and walked over to the couch, only to toss me on it. "Touch me," he ordered.

"No! I can't! Oh, you big, bad, Viking man!" It was hard to not smile during this game. "Oh, let me go and pillage elsewhere!"

With my hands still trapped in his grasp, he held them above my head and kissed me fiercely. His tongue glided along my lips and then thrust into my mouth. I kissed him back with more intensity. Tyb's mouth moved from my lips to my neck and then down until he captured my pert nipple and suckled hard. I writhed on the couch under his assault. His hand slacked enough for him to release one of my mitts, and then he guided me to his cock. I needed no prompting and caressed the length of him, silently delighting in the bead of excitement from his cock's tip that made my handling of him slick.

Tyb let go of my other hand long enough to rip the panties right off me, then captured it again. He moved from kneeling next to the couch to pinning both hands above my head again and sliding into my heat. Slowly, slowly, he pushed forth until he could sink no deeper.

With my hands held hostage, I writhed and wiggled, trying to dislodge him from my pussy. Didn't work. He tightened his grasp and began fucking me in earnest. I wrapped my legs around his waist and crossed my ankles to lock him in.

Tyb whispered, "You okay?"

"Oh God yes! Fuck me Tyb!" I arched my back with hopes he's pay pointed attention to my breasts again. Instead, he plundered my lips. I moaned into the cavern of his mouth, and Tyb rewarded me with breaking off the kiss and letting go of my hands to caress my body.

He moved his grasp to my hips and said, "Watch Izzy. I want you to watch."

I opened my eyes and looked down to see Tyb's rock hard cock slide out of me. He grasped the shaft with his hands and rubbed the tip on my aching clit. I bucked my hips, willing him to fuck me some more. With a haze of lust, I focused on the veiny length of his cock stretching me wide.

Couldn't hold back any longer. I thrashed beneath him, murmuring his name as a Holy litany against the dark oppression of unfulfillment.

Tyb gave in to my passionate plea for completion. I could feel him pulsate inside me, and I loved the sensation.

"I like this game."

He lay atop me, spent. "I like this game too." Tyb looked in my eyes before asking, "You okay? I didn't hurt you, did I?"

"I'm fine. And in round two, I'm going to be the Valkyrie and you will be the blacksmith. I'm gonna want some pointed attention with your *sword*."

"Don't let me like you too much, Izzy."

"Too late." He didn't reply, but I could tell by his reaction that I spoke the truth. I didn't bother to tell him that I liked him way too much, already. So instead, I settled for kissing him stupid and having my way with his eager body.

Dinner got burnt.

Chapter Twenty-Two

It was two months before we heard from Mara again. In that span of time, twice Tyb had gone down the mountain for a day, leaving me in charge. Also, I discovered many things about my new life. For example, cheese isn't as easy as it sounds to make and scalding the milk gives the cheese an off-flavor. Oh! And did you know rabbits can conceive anytime they mate? As in the act of sex causes a doe rabbit to ovulate. Imagine getting pregnant every time you got laid. I felt worse for those animals than when I first found out Tyb ate them.

We were in his Mule, heading through the forest when he asked, "How squeamish are you?"

"Why, about to get man-gross and I need to avert my eyes?"

"No. I have to transfer some rabbits for processing."

I quirked my brow. "*Processing*?"

"One could say 'harvest' or 'slaughter' or 'butcher' if that makes a difference."

"You want me to help kill rabbits." I stated it as fact although my voice held a note of disbelief.

"No. I would like you there for company." Tyb stopped the Mule. "Sad fact of having an omnivore diet means critters are going to die. If I'm going to eat, I have to kill, distasteful as it is. Having company to distract from an otherwise sucky job would be nice. If you don't want to be there, I totally understand. I can drop you back off at the house when I head to the processing station."

I had very mixed feelings about Tyb's request. On one hand, it's good to know where one's food comes from. My time on the homestead so far has taught me not to take simple luxuries like food for granted. Now, I have a damn good measure of what it takes to put dinner on the table and let me tell you, supermarket shopping is a great buffer for the reality of where that food came from.

On the other hand, there's the whole killing a bunny thing.

"Is there a lot of blood?" I asked. Blood could be a good excuse not to witness the slaughter of innocent rabbits.

"No. I use cervical dislocation, so it's quick, clean and if done correctly, painless to the animal. They are giving their life to sustain mine. I owe them a good death, stupid as it sounds."

"Doesn't sound stupid." Sounds like he didn't like making creatures suffer. That's decent.

We arrived at the rabbit colony. A wire fence surrounded a chunk of land with a small hill in the center. Tyb climbed out of the Mule and grabbed a dog crate from the cargo area. He stepped over the fence, turned and beckoned for me to follow. I did so, not sure what I'd see on this adventure. Until today, the rabbits had been a chore Tyb didn't share. On the hill's far side, there sat a wire cage holding five rabbits. Other rabbits were grazing on what looked to be squares of overgrown sod in the main paddock area. Tyb was at the cage, unfastening the top. Once it was off, he reached in and lifted one of the gray rabbits out to put in the dog crate.

"What breed are those?" I asked. Didn't look like the English Angora I had as a kid, that's for certain. Looked around and noticed PVC pipes leading into the hillside. There were at least eight tunnels.

"These are a Giant Chinchilla and New Zealand mix."

After all the rabbits were transferred from the cage to the crate, Tyb walked back to the Mule and I followed. Gently, he placed the crate in the cargo area and covered it with a canvas tarp. "To keep the wind off them. I don't like the rabbits getting worked up."

We hopped in and drove at a very sedate pace (for Tyb, that is) down a hill, toward the far end of his grain meadow. There was an old lichen covered pine tree. Next to it, a tall stump with a smooth top. Next to the stump, what looked like a Cabela's camping special—an outdoor kitchen. Well, the sink and counter part of an outdoor kitchen. I could see running from the hillside behind the processing station a PVC pipe, angled to the meadow, with water flowing out the visible end.

We stopped by the large tree and as I looked up, I saw a four foot long board, about eight inches wide screwed to one of the lower branches, which just happened to be right overhead. There was a V cut and smoothed on one end of the board. When I returned my gaze to Tyb, I saw him moving the crate from the Mule to next to the tree, then fill up two five gallon buckets I didn't notice hiding underneath the camp-sink. He placed the buckets next to the stump.

Tyb started talking as he opened the crate and removed a rabbit. "I try to handle them every day so they get used to me. The first year I raised rabbits was very informative of what *not* to do. I didn't handle them, didn't want to get attached to them. They'd run from me and wouldn't eat their fodder until I left the paddock. And when I did get a hold of one, it'd scream. I fucking hate rabbit screams."

"Sounds like the rabbits knew what was coming."

"It's what I got for not giving them the respect they deserved. I still don't name the rabbits, but I try to have them accustomed to being handled." Tyb now had the rabbit in his arms, petting it from ears to tail. "This is the part you probably don't want to watch, Izzy."

I didn't turn around as he slid the rabbit's head into the V of that board I eyeballed earlier. With the rabbit's head on one side and the body on the other, Tyb supported the creature. He closed his eyes and drew a deep breath. The rabbit wasn't upset or fighting. Just placidly accepting the awkward position it found itself. Tyb gave the hind legs a quick jerk, and the rabbit instantly went limp.

"That was quicker than I thought it'd be…" I trailed off, not sure what to say exactly. Tyb's expression was far more expressive than anything I could vocalize. It wasn't disgust on his face, but it was apparent that he took no joy in the job at hand. "So, change of topic?" I asked with as upbeat a tone I could muster.

"That would be a welcome diversion."

It was my turn to take a deep breath. I'd been giving

Mara's idea a lot of thought. While my two months up here bordered on bucolic, I knew I'd never be truly at peace until Christos got handled once and for all. If that meant I'd be skinned alive, fine. Two months away from him was worth it. It was worth knowing that sex can be fun for both parties and not be vanilla. It was worth knowing that not all kinky guys are abusive. It was worth knowing how sweet freedom could taste.

"So, I've been thinking. I want to fuck with Christos. I like your idea, and the fact is even though he's not here, I'll always feel his presence until I know for certain he's gone—whatever that fate may be. The proviso for the porn thing is that we'd have to do it within the next couple weeks, because I'm going to run out of my pills soon."

Tyb stopped what he was doing and turned to face me. "Are you sure? Once they are on the internet, there's no going back."

"It'll be Selesta on the internet, not Izzy." I won't deny the cocky tone in my voice. "He wants to skin me? I will give him a good goddamn reason to get mad, and then I want to kick him in the jimmy for being a dick. Figuratively, of course." I smiled.

His eyes searched mine for a long moment. "We need to make a plan when we get back to the house. It's almost October. If Aisha is stuck on the Isle of Twilight, then getting to her in winter seas will be difficult. I need to call Mara tonight, need to hammer out an outline. You don't have to do this, Izzy. We can go the suggestive route rather than hardcore."

"I want hardcore. Not because it'll piss him off, but because I enjoy your version of *hardcore.*" I didn't realize until I spoke how true that was.

"Let's finish discussing this when we get back home. It's kind of awkward, harvesting rabbit and talking about sex and vengeance.

"You said to distract you." *Remember, Tyb?*

He turned back around and got back to work, skinning the rabbit. "Too much of a distraction, I'm afraid."

"That's because you're sprung on me." I knew he was by how some days he'd avoid me—not rudely, but there was always something calling to be done. If his rocket mass heater is so damned efficient, why keep cutting all that wood when he already has three times the amount needed to heat through winter?

"I try not to think about it, Izzy."

"Why? I like to think about it. You're a sweet and decent guy. It's almost sad that you're stuck up here, alone more often than not."

"I'm not always alone. You forget the other strays Mara has dragged here. And family."

"So you admit you don't miss the company of women?" I half-scoffed at the notion.

"I didn't say *that*. I just said I'm not always alone. You're proof of that."

"I know that. But when this whole thing with Christos ends… I…I… I just want to thank you, Tyb, for everything."

"Everything? You're working off the room and board by helping out here. Don't thank me for the hard work you do."

I bit my lip in frustration. "You don't know how empowering the past two months have been for me."

"Because I'm *sprung* on you?" Tyb teased.

"That's a bonus." I grinned, even though his broad back faced me. "You're the best vacation I've ever had. That's saying something for someone who has traveled around the globe." Cue the perverted passport stamp joke.

"Just admit it, Izzy. You think I'm hot and you lust for me every waking moment, and make your toes curl in anticipation."

"There's that too. But I…" I wanted to tell him when this was all over, and if the world didn't get salted by exploding nuclear zompires… what? That I wanted to stay up here, working with him? That I am way more fond of him than I have any right to be? That I wanted to know if he could picture me in the future, *his future*?"

"What are you trying to tell me?" His back still faced me. "I know you care a lot for me, Izzy. Just don't. Last thing I want to do is hurt you."

"You won't intentionally hurt me. I know that." I couldn't shut up, despite my brain screeching for the vocal brakes. "You know what's sad? I was married two years to Christos and never had the level of trust with him that I do with you. That saddens me."

"I have no words of consolation. It is what it is." I watched him shrug his shoulders. "*Woulda coulda shoulda…* it's a poison to a happy life. "

I needed to know, needed a definitive answer. "How soon do you want me to leave once this thing with Christos is settled?" My affection for Tyb could spell bad things if I have nothing else to focus on. Chores took care of that during the day, but by night my mind wanders toward questions I have no answer.

"You want to leave?" I never heard that tone from Tyb. Surprise, tinged with hurt.

"No. I like it up here *way* too much, I think."

"Too much as in you want to get back to normalcy? Or too much as in you want to stay up here longer?"

I worried my lower lip with my teeth before answering. "Very much the staying up here part."

Slowly, Tyb turned around to face me. "I truly wish that was an option, Izzy."

I flinched at his reply, honest as it was. "Why?"

"You don't want to know the answer to that."

"Uh, yes I do. I just asked why."

"Have it your way. You staying up here isn't an option for longer than necessary because you have family who would love nothing more than to hear from you again. When Haytham is out of the picture, I would hope you'd comfort your family who thinks you're dead. I don't know how long you'll be up here, but I can't keep you to myself. As much as I have enjoyed our time together, fact is your family has dibs on you."

"My family would want me happy."

"At their expense?"

"Damn it, Tyb. It's not black and white. Family and you. That's a nice combination."

His tone and eyes implored me to be reasonable. "Don't love me, Izzy."

I gave him a wistful smile. "Too late, Tyb."

Chapter Twenty-Three

"First off, follow the protocol I laid out in that first package I sent you, Tyb. That'll give you access to a series of proxy servers. Those will block any attempt to root out your IP address and get a lock on your location. Best part, those proxies are run by either the CIA or FBI. They have a vested interest in keeping tabs on Haytham, more so now with that damned explosion. They have your back. It's up to you guys to find the sites to play on. After you make your, uh, *message*, upload to a site and then text Haytham the URL. He'll watch, get pissed, then order his cronies to hack. Then you'll post the next message at a different site, so on and so forth. Spread them out every other day. It'll be often enough to get his attention in a big way." Mara was on speakerphone, while Tyb and I sat at the kitchen table, making notes of her orders. "Uh, Izzy?"

"Here."

"You need to create an online persona."

"Okay. Can do." I already put thought into what my "stage name" would be. One of the things I appreciated most about Tyb was that no matter what I suggested, he'd be game. I suspected he'd get a kick out of my suggestion. "Anything else?"

"Just get cracking. I've got inside help to take down Haytham, but we have a very limited window before the East Siberian Sea will be impossible to traverse."

I gasped. "Siberia?"

"Yeah. Tiny island. Back in the day, the Soviets established a polar base there. A big portion of the island is a glacier. Ice packs are gnarly. "

"That'd be the Isle of Twilight?" I asked, already knowing the answer.

"Yep. That's what Haytham named it when he brokered a deal with the Russians for its exclusive use. Was called Henrietta Island before. So, you guys work on the distraction, I'll be working on the taking his ass down part. Instructions are in the box, Tyb. Just set it up as detailed and everything will be cool. Don't mess up the proxy information. Izzy, use the phone I gave you to send the messages. Haytham can't track it. Spy phones don't release GPS data, so that'll piss him off. Three weeks, tops. We need to be in there before the middle of October. Gotta go." *Click.*

I turned to Tyb. "I need to order a wig. Needs to look like my old haircut. Lingerie, too. You… you'll need a mask or something to hide your face."

"Halloween themed?"

"No. I just don't want Christos to know it's you. I…I… I don't want him coming after you."

"You're to be bait, Izzy, not a martyr. He'll come after both of us. He'll kill me first, then take his time with you if he manages to get a hold of us. I think that's unlikely, but, still. If that's what it gets down to, that's how it'll play out."

"Are you positive about that?" I sure as hell don't want Tyb dying for me. My pussy can't be that magical.

"Think about it. Take out the biggest threat first, that way you don't have to worry about being interrupted."

"Don't die for me. Promise me you won't."

Tyb's voice lowered into a very somber tone. "I will make no such promise."

I needed to know if his prophetic visions played any part in this new adventure. "Did you have any dreams about this?"

Tyb shook his head in the negative, while those warm amber eyes regarded me warily. "No."

"Just no dying. Your goats would miss you." I tried eking out a smile, but couldn't quite get it.

Tyb shrugged his broad shoulders. "At least I'd be remembered fondly."

"True." I sat up straight and smiled super-wide as I switched topics. "So, I have a tentative battle plan."

Tyb's brow quirked. "Do you now?"

"Oh yeah. And I know it'll catch his attention because it'll incorporate kink. And the name alone will piss him off."

"You've chosen already?"

Couldn't resist laughing. "I've been thinking about it a while." How would I get back at the man who threatened me? Who deliberately hurt me? Yeah, I put perhaps too much time into comeuppance, but fucker deserves it. Starting with our wedding night, supposedly one of the most romantic days of my life. Ha. What a joke. Forced to one's knees, made to say demeaning words and embrace a *master.* To kiss torture implements and say *thank you* after every lash. Once, I thought about cutting Christos' throat as he slept. The only thing which kept me from traveling down that path was what would happen if I failed to kill him. He'd come back and torture me to death, I knew it. I needed my closure from my marriage. Deep in my gut, I knew that the closure came at a price—my death or Christos'.

Tyb's voice broke through my thoughts. "Evidently. So lay it on me."

I cleared my throat. "*Mrs. Haytham's Fantasies…* How does that sound? Every message will be you costumed differently." His eyebrows rose even more when I mentioned costumed. "I want to make cuckold porn. I want that dirt bag to see me getting freaky, I want him pissed, I want him dead. "

Tyb started laughing hard. "Oh, you mean to piss in his eye and tell him it's raining. Me in different costumes… each one is a separate man you're cheating with. That's some major shit."

I lit up. He was spot on. "Exactly. Got fatigues and camo makeup? I like that idea a lot. Just a lot of kinky role play. I'll moan how much I love your cock and how glad I am that my husband is busy at the lab so I can play with all these strange men who all happen to have your build." I giggled. I liked that thought. I could go for a gang bang of Tybs, I think.

"You have a penchant for vindictiveness, don't you?" He eyeballed me hard, a small smile on his lips.

"No. Just a lower tolerance toward bullshit propagated by those who claimed to love me. I think I've come to realize how angry I am at him for all he did to me." Because that fucker did a lot to undermine my sense of self-worth, accomplishment, and safety.

"I know he was no cake walk for you. I don't even want to imagine what he's putting Aisha through."

"Yeah, that thought has crossed my mind, too. I wouldn't wish him on my worst enemy." I sighed and changed the topic. "Never asked before, but are Mara and Aisha identical twins?"

"No. Fraternal. Mara has blue eyes, black hair. Aisha has brown hair and green eyes. Mara and I take after our father, Aisha takes after our mother in appearance."

Well, that's good that they don't look alike. It didn't occur to me when I found out Mara's sister was my husband –err—ex-husband's lover. Had they been identical twins… Oh I shudder to think how Christos would have reacted to Mara and me upon that revelation. "So this should be over by October… I don't know what I'm going to do after."

Another shrug of his shoulders. "Start over. Chart a new life. Find an adventure and live it."

I wanted to tell him I had already done that, here, with him. Couldn't though. Tyb was absolutely resolute that I stay with my family as soon as I can, they needed me more, to know I'm well, than he does. While he's right, that fucking stings.

"I could relocate anywhere, couldn't I?"

"You'll need some serious cash… but I can help you out with that. Adventure tomorrow."

"What kind of adventure?"

"The kind I don't tell people."

"That sounds ominous."

Tyb leaned back in his chair. "In a very good way, Izzy. Ever been gold panning before?"

I shook my head in the negative. "Never." People still go prospecting?

"I happen to know a very nice spot, not too far. The nuggets I've pulled from there have funded my life quite nicely. You've built up some muscle… so whatever you can carry back home from the gold mine is yours to keep. There's a fellow in Covelo that buys gold. At almost two grand an ounce, it's a good way to make some cash." Tyb cracked a smile that didn't quite reach his eyes. "Whatever may come, I want you prepared and taken care of. If I die, you can stay here. I emailed my dad and let him know. He can show you the way down the mountain."

"Why do you keep thinking you're going to die?" His fixation on the subject bothered me. "I don't know if I could stay up here without you."

"You know the basics of survival up here. You'd do well. You'd be safe." Tyb's voice was assured, calming, and to me, seemed to hold a touch of longing.

I'd be intensely lonely up here, without him. "And you think zompires are going to get us all?" Why else would I need to be protected in a world where Christos Haytham no longer existed? "Besides, would I really be safe up here if your sister—my husband's mistress—found out I was living in her brother's home? No matter how long I'd live here, it'd always be *your* house."

He wasn't willing to discuss. "Well, good thing we'll make you fiscally solvent tomorrow so you can move back to civilization and mingle with normal people."

"You, my dear Tyb, are remarkably normal in extraordinary circumstances."

"You're too generous."

"No I'm not. I'm selfish. I can admit it."

"Not as selfish as me, I'm sure of that."

"You don't have a selfish bone in your body, Tyb."

He tilted his head back and laughed. "Oh, I do too. And right now it's hard as a rock for you."

Chapter Twenty-Four

I will say that making internet porn is *interesting*.

Mara sent Tyb a selection of high-definition video cameras, tripods, lights and reflectors, and software for the computer. Another package contained thumb drives and a handful of paper, all detailing IPs, Proxy information, Passwords, details for connecting to a secure Navy satellite for a new internet connection and contact email addresses for not just FBI and CIA, but the Department of Homeland Defense and the Pentagon as well.

Tyb installed the software to secure the connection while I unpacked the small cameras and slim tripods. Three cameras, total. One completely secure connection later, and we were in business.

The porn biz, that is. Oh, my parents would be proud, I'm sure.

We didn't use a script. I laid out my gimmick, a frustrated housewife who would 'film' her indiscretions as a fuck you to her workaholic husband. Sometimes the truth can be a caricature, much like my marriage. We filmed in Tyb's room since it was larger and had the computer. Also included in the box were a set of white sheets, with a note written in Sharpie on the outside, reading 'P*ut this on your fuck zones. For software, you'll see.*'

Our first attempt was an adventure. We turned the cameras on and took our positions. I lay atop the snowy white flannel on the bed while Tyb waited in the living room.

Tyb came busting in his door, wearing camouflage pants and boots. Shirtless, his torso muscles rippled underneath the strategically placed compact flood lights. His face smudged with green, brown, and black, seemed to make his eyes glitter with a dangerous gleam.

I wore a white cotton camisole that reached the tops of my thighs, and nothing else. Sat up and faked surprise. "You came! I don't know when my husband will be back, but oh! Fuck me, *Philippe*! I want that horse cock I know you have hiding for me." Every time Tyb and I make one of these Fuck You messages, I was going to call him by another name.

Tyb lost his composure for a moment after I said *horse cock*. His teeth, startling white against his face paint, showed his amusement when he smiled. "I'm AWOL right now. I knew you'd be wet, waiting for me." He started unbuttoning his pants to reveal a trail of hair leading south. "Want to know what I've been thinking of every night?"

I arose from the bed and sauntered his way, only to wrap my arms around his neck and nibble on his chin. "Tell me you've been thinking about me sucking your cock, because that's constantly on my mind." True, too.

He rewarded me with another smile and lifted me up as he walked to the bed. He set me down in front of a camera at the bed's foot, and Tyb stepped away. I loved the view. His cock was hard and peeping up from the waistband of his fatigues. I'm just saying, I probably should have practiced unzipping his pants with my teeth. Oh well, edit that out later. I went to town licking his shaft that I didn't notice for a couple minutes that he was holding a camcorder for a POV shot of me giving him head. I tried giving him my best sloe-eyed look as I licked the bottom of his cock, from balls to tip. Tyb spoke, his voice as rich with lust. "Tell me what you want, Selesta."

I'm sure for a moment I looked dumbfounded. Never before has he addressed me by my real name and it felt weird and a bit forced on his part. But once I got my equilibrium again, the most wickedest idea came to me. With one hand, I worked Tyb's shaft, and the other meandered south to tease my clit. "Mmmm, all I want from you Philippe, is some jewelry."

Tyb quirked his eyebrow and echoed, "Jewelry? What kind of bling does my naughty housewife want? I'm only on a soldier's salary, so if you want diamonds, better ask your husband."

I rubbed the tip of Tyb's cock around on my lips, enjoying

the throbbing shaft in my hand. "I don't want diamonds." *Lick.* "Besides, my husband won't ever give me what I want… I want pearls. A pearl necklace." With that, I began sucking and licking Tyb, while working him with my hand. He tilted his head back and moaned low, in such a way that sent tiny, snowboarding snowmen down my spine in delight. "You can afford a pearl necklace, *right*?"

"I'd give you a pearl necklace any time you ask."

I let go of Tyb's joystick and whipped my camisole over my head. "I'm asking for one now. Before my husband comes back." I licked my lips.

Tyb, ever the sex-magician, gave me what I asked for. Hot spurts covered my neck and breasts. "You're a bad girl, Mrs. Haytham. Will you show your new pearls to your husband?"

"No, he wouldn't appreciate them."

Tyb smacked my ass. "He doesn't know what he's missing."

After that, we turned off the flood lights, I hit the shower while Tyb went to the computer to survey our first attempt at making porn for Christos' eyes. By the miracle of software, using one still camera and the POV shot, and Mara's photos of what once was my home with Christos, oh, it looked like I was sucking Tyb off at the foot of my marital bed in my gilded cage. That would piss my dear, delusional ex off, hopefully incite him to recklessness and lower his guard, the thought of me fooling around with various men in our home while he was away at work.

Hell hath no fury like a wife abused and resenting it…

The first porn site we choose had over ten million members—paying members. Webcam shots of my fake ID verified I was over the age of 18 to the satisfaction of the porn site admin. After having my membership approved, the video got uploaded. Every megabyte transferred through the proxy servers made my heart beat a bit faster than before. Then it was done. I looked to Tyb when he clicked on the vid to fetch the URL. I had my cell in hand, typing in the web address to text. I wrote, *You need to see what Selesta did.*

Pushed send, and away it went via satellite connection.

Tyb went to the bathroom to clean up and I sat with the

cellphone Zamara gave me, resting on my bare knee. Christos fulfilled my expectation with a quick and indignant reply.

Who are you and how did you get this number?

I smirked as I wrote, *Someone who knows Selesta and her secrets.*

HOW DID YOU GET THIS NUMBER?

Tyb walked in on my chortling like a teenager while typing my response. *Selli told me. Watch the vid at link I sent you. She says you'll like it.*

My wife is dead.

When I read that, I laughed. "Oh am I? Think again, asshole."

You sure about that? I have it on good authority she's quite happy being away from you. How's the Siberian Sea, by the way? Can't be as nice as Northern California. Selli would tell you to kiss her ass, but she doesn't speak crazy person.

Whoever this is, I will kill you after I kill my wife again, if she were alive.

I thought, HA! Not if I get you first. *Come on, Haytham. Where's your sense of wonder at seeing the woman you married getting off with a gigantic cock? Besides, do you really want to document your intention to commit a felony? Don't you know you're always being watched?*

Chapter Twenty-Five

I WILL GIVE YOU ONE CHANCE TO TELL ME WHO YOU ARE BEFORE I FIND OUT MYSELF AND RIP YOUR SPINE OUT YOUR ASS WHEN I TRACK YOU DOWN.

I was rather enjoying my game of Fuck You Text Messages. Being away from him and his physical presence gave me an audacity I never felt before. *You couldn't keep tabs on Selesta, what makes you think you can find me? You won't be able to get a lock on my position via GPS coordinates. Face it, buckaroo, without your crack IT team, you're nothing but a rich jizz stain on society.*

ARE YOU THE MAN IN THAT VIDEO WITH MY WIFE? I WILL FUCKING GUT YOU.

No. I'm not a tauntaun and you are no Han Solo. Maybe Hand Solo, at best. I'm the female Selli likes to sleep with at night. I keep her snuggly and safe.

LIAR.

You'd know all about liars, wouldn't you, Christos? Still have your testicles, or has the Siberian cold neutered you?

Tyb read over my shoulder and whistled low. "Jesus, Izzy. Going for the nuts? Low blow."

"Having his masculinity questioned always angered him. When I suggested I had better reading comprehension than he, because you know, I worked in publishing and it was kinda my job to understand that which I am reading, Christos backhanded me. Then… it was a night I wish I could forget, Tyb. The first of many nights I wish I could forget, or at least pretend didn't happen. I will talk mad shit to Christos now that he can't hurt me tonight, and I'll say all the shit I've kept bottled up. He's earned an earful, would be a shame to keep him from knowing not all are in awe of his wealth or intellect." *Vir caput est mulieris.* I hate that phrase. Latin for 'Man is head of the woman." The phrase Christos would utter every time he punished me. The phase I needed to use as a mantra during punishment to appease the madman I married. *Vir caput est mulieris,* the song of my anguish and dehumanization.

"Has he replied yet?"

"No. He's angry now. He's brainstorming retribution, I bet." Stewing and mulling and boiling in anger. In hindsight, I hoped Christos didn't take his anger out on Aisha, but instead directed it toward finding the one mocking him.

"Well, tomorrow is another day. It's late and I'm tired. Sorry to put off gold panning to accomplish this," Tyb swept his arm around in a grand gesture towards cameras and lights on tripods. "Did you still want to go?"

"Yeah, I'm interested in playing a '49er." I started putting the photo gear away. Tyb stored the boxes under his bed. When that was done, I meandered to my room, white cotton chemise in hand, and slipped into bed nude.

Damn dreams.

Rough hands grabbed me by the hair, did things… Stop! No! That voice, no…Say it!… Vir caput est mulieris! Vir caput est mulieris! Please! Stop now! Please! You are the master, you are my master, without you I am nothing… No, not the paddle! I said the words…No, I will never leave you…I hate you… please stop! Please! No, don't put the plastic bag over my head again, I'll be good! I promise! I love you! Why are you doing this to me? Please! You said you loved me! Why….. Vir caput est mulieris!

Tyb's voice woke me. "Izzy, you okay?" He stood in the doorway to my room, hands braced against the doorjamb.

Groggy and tired, I replied, "Don't know." I felt like crying. The first time he hit me was three weeks after the wedding. I was secure in the thought that, *yay married life!* Was just as cool as the honeymoon period. It wasn't. My honeymoon was a mask Christos wore. The real Christos came out overtime. First, slowly. But then it was like a toilet paper roll; the further along we got, the faster it seemed Christos seemed to cycle between his moods of kindness and generosity to vicious and evil.

Me tormenting Christos has a side effect of tormenting myself as well. "Christos will kill me first chance he gets. I guaranteed that tonight when I sent him the text messages." I tried suppressing a shudder.

"He won't kill you." Tyb meandered from the door to my bed. He sat down on the side. "Were you dreaming of him?"

"Yes. I was dreaming of him and his many shades of being fucked up in the head." And wishing it was all a dream and not based whatsoever in reality.

"Can I get you anything? Water?"

"No, I'm fine. Well, I'm not… but I think once this is over and I know he's no longer a threat to me, I'll be very fine indeed." Or dead, and I wouldn't care.

"How about a hug?"

The man sitting on my bed is pure Kryptonite. "A hug sounds good."

I sat up more while Tyb leaned over to engulf me in a gentle bear hug. I wrapped my arms around his neck and squeezed. Hugs are awesomely healing.

Tyb's phone rang, splitting us apart. "It's two in the morning. Whoever is calling, is calling for a good reason." He left my room to fetch his cell. He was speaking on nit when he came back into my room. "Okay Mara, I'm going to put you on speakerphone. You tell us both what's going on." He pressed a button and set the phone face down on my bed.

Zamara's voice echoed in the room. "Whatever you guys did, it worked. He and Aisha have left the Isle of Twilight earlier today. In fact, they are off the coast in Noyo harbor, using really bad fake IDs as a mister and missus Valtoris, renting a houseboat. However, with a face as recognizable as Haytham's, especially with his mug blasted on every television for a couple months, it didn't work. He was detained by the sheriff."

"It's over?" The words were out of my mouth before I realized it.

Zamara laughed. "I wish. Was able to convince local law enforcement that he is, indeed, Claud Valtoris. So he's on the loose. Aisha, she's still in jail, but at least she's safe there."

"Why didn't she get bailed out?" Tyb asked, his voice dark with building anger.

"She tried cutting Haytham's throat. Her first generation implant is failing and she's getting hungry."

"So that's the news?" I asked.

"No. The news is that Aisha bit Haytham. So he's in a hurry to find you. He doesn't have his full lab anymore. Everything got taken for evidence at the Washington state lab. He doesn't have an implant to slow down the Virteria Serum. So there's a live bomb on its way to find you guys."

Tyb spoke again, his tone calmer. "So, it's on like Donkey Kong?"

"Yes, sir."

"What are you doing?"

"I'm on my way to Aisha. Need to ask her something. You guys, go make friends with the tree house—or at least start moving your root cellar in there. No telling how long you'll be on lockdown. There's a taskforce assigned to take Haytham down, alive, if possible. Don't put yourselves in harm's way. Stay low and keep an ear to the ground. I'll talk to you again when I have more information." She hung up.

It was there, in the silence which lingered, when I realized my nightmare had only just begun this night.

Chapter Twenty-Six

By moonlight and lantern, Tyb and I filled the back of the Mule with boxes of his canned goods. "I'll be gone in the morning. Going to take my critters down the mountain to Bucky's." Bucky is the pig-farming, rabbit-fur trading neighbor. "Shouldn't be gone long, just a couple hours."

I didn't like the thought of being up here alone with Christos running lose. In fact, that was deeply unsettling. The look on my face must have been epic for Tyb to tack on, "You'll have the dogs with you too, Izzy. You'll be fine." He then offered me a smile.

"What should I do while you're gone?"

"I'll show you. Come on." We walked back to the house and went into his bedroom. He opened the secret door to the panic room and told me to follow. Anxiety heightened my awareness, that maybe in a few hours I'd be scurrying down this corridor and hiding in fear of the man who has haunted my world far too long. How stupid and inexperienced was I when I got involved with him? Damn hindsight.

When we reached the panic room we went through the door leading to the treehouse. It was a long walk in darkness until we reached the safety of the mini castle. We walked past the room where Tyb removed my implant to the next door.

"This is what you can do." Tyb opened the door and revealed several closed circuit camera monitors, all focused on the outdoors. There was no feed from the house or panic room. "Keep an eye out. Anyone you don't recognize is probably going to be on the taskforce."

"And if I see Christos…?" Sit here and hide? Do nothing and wait for the cowboys to save me? I didn't like the thought of sitting around and doing jack shit but get my anxiety going.

Tyb looked at me in a manner I never noticed before. "What do you want to do?"

"Not freak out."

He cracked a smile. "That's a good start. You got a couple options. Sit tight and let the task force handle him or defend yourself if he's that close to you."

Could I shoot Christos? Putting a bullet through a can is a lot different than putting one through flesh. *I suppose I could imagine his torso as can of Dr. Pepper and let loose...*

"Guns are in the house. Should we go back and get them?" I asked, half-wondering if my revolver would do the job.

"Oh, Izzy. I'm prepared." He turned around and shut the door to the monitor room. Behind the door, a large metal locker set into the wall. He opened the locker and revealed an arsenal that couldn't possibly be legal.

At least a dozen long guns, half of which looked like assault guns with banana clips. Tyb reached in and pulled two out, one much larger than the other. "This is your gun. Make friends and follow me." He held out the smaller of the two to me. I expected it to weigh a lot more than it did when I took it from his hands.

"That's a Saiga. Less than ten pounds. This here is my Vera Barrett," he held aloft the huge fucking gun. "This is thirty-two pounds."

"Are they legal?"

"As long as they have a ten-round clip, yep. Any larger and it's heavily frowned upon in California."

"Are we in frowny territory?"

He laughed. "Completely, utterly, totally. Thirty round capacity suits my needs. Don't have to reload as often."

"But it'll take longer to reload."

"True, but if one takes out the target first, the need to reload is reduced."

"Point taken, Gun Guru."

With a metal box about the size of two stacked bricks in one hand, and his 'Vera' in the other, Tyb led me out of the room and down the corridor to yet another door. It revealed a set of stairs, which we climbed in silence. At the top, yet another door. That lead us to the top of the tree house. Ragged columns of concrete rose around us, giving the appearance of a stump rotted and darkened by age. "Up here, you can get a damn good view of the property." Kinda hard to tell, being that dawn had yet to make its approach this morning. Must be four-thirty. All was quiet in the land, with the exception of a lonely owl hooting every so often. No moon tonight, just the shimmering of stars overhead.

"Did you hear that?" Tyb whispered.

"No. What was it?" I asked back, just as quiet.

"Sticks breaking. Listen."

And so I did, straining my ears to hear whatever put Tyb on alert.

I didn't hear what set him off, but I did see a light in the distance. "What's that?" In the darkness I pointed, but it did no good. Vague outline of an extended index finger at best.

"Hold on, I'll be right back." Tyb leaned his gun against the wall and went back down the stairs at a quick pace. He returned shortly, carrying what looked kinda like binoculars. He handed me a pair. "Here, night vision."

I slipped the night vision goggles on over my head. Tyb turned them on and everything took on a green cast. "Do not look at the light. It'll blind you. Look above the light and see the face. Left hand side of the goggles has a dial. Turn it forward to zoom in."

"It's a woman. Not Zamara. The dogs seem to know her."

"Fuck. It's Aisha." Tyb's voice softened as he realized who it was.

"How did she get out of jail?"

"I don't know. But if she's infected with the Virteria Serum, she's dangerous. She cannot be trusted."

"On the bright side, she attacked Christos. That's got to count for something." Too bad she didn't rip his head off. That would have been awesome.

"That's because she's dangerous. She wouldn't bite the hand that's been feeding her... but now, that's not so certain." Deep resignation sat heavy in Tyb's voice.

I leaned my gun next to Vera and gave Tyb a hug. "I'm sorry shit is sucking right now." I brought this upon him. That didn't sit well.

Tyb placed a kiss to the top of my head and said, "Shit was bound to happen sometime. Just do not trust Aisha. Do not get close to her."

Sarcastically, I asked, "Want me to keep a gun pointing at her at all times, too?"

If Tyb used sarcasm, it didn't register with me. "Probably a prudent idea."

"It's your sister!" But if it came down to it, whose life would he preserve?

"If it were Haytham, I'd be saying the same thing. They both are dangerous, Haytham more so now."

The light in the distance neared. "What do we do? Let her go up to the house and think we're there? Call her out when she gets here? What's the plan, captain?"

"I wish I fucking knew."

Chapter Twenty-Seven

Aisha trudged her way to the tree house. Tyb kept his gun aimed at her the entire time. Finally, when she crossed through the meadow, she arrived at the foot of the tree house. Made me wonder if it was her plan to sneak onto the property without Tyb knowing. "Hey you two! Let me in."

She could see us? She wasn't wearing any sort of image enhancing device that I could see. Tyb called down, "What are you doing here, Aisha?"

"Came to see my big brother. And use that room you have set aside for me. I, uh, broke up with my boyfriend."

"Who bailed you out of jail?"

"You knew about that? Mom and Dad. All I had to do was tell them I broke up with him and was going to see you… they arranged it all."

"They've missed you."

"Yeah, I know. So you gonna let me in or are you planning on the bears and mountain lions to off me first?"

"Aisha, I know you are not safe to be around. If I were to let you in, there will be at least one gun pointed at you at all times. I cannot trust you."

"Well, that's not exactly the homecoming I remember…"

"Little Sister, I can see you twinkling in the night. I'm not even wearing night vision. There is something not right with you and its Haytham's fault. I heard you took a bite out of him, so now he's going glitter alongside you."

"Know what happens if I bite him again? Your little home away from reality will exist no longer. That can be arranged, ya know."

"Since when do you channel Don Corleone?"

"Since my brother's been acting like a suspicious douche. Just a heads up, Haytham is coming this way. He doesn't know how to get here like me, but he'll follow my trail and be here, probably in a couple hours. He's no good without a GPS telling him where to go."

I spoke up. "So Morgan isn't with him to guide the way?"

"No, he's still stuck in the cold. Fucking Siberia is cold. But the fossils laying around were a nice bonus."

Tyb spoke up again. "Are you really split from Haytham? No pulling my chain, Aisha."

"He and I had a big disagreement. Major, as in me taking a knife to his junk." Aisha's bubbly demeanor seemed at odds with how I pictured her. That's what I get for making assumptions.

After a moment, Tyb spoke. "Give me a couple minutes and I'll open the house. Just… don't do anything stupid. That's not a phone call I want to make to Mom and Dad."

"Aye aye, captain. I can save you the trip. You gotta see what I can do now." Aisha took a few steps backward before running at full speed—no, faster than full speed- toward the treehouse. Somehow, she ran up the side and jumped up high at the last moment to vault over the cement battlements, joining Tyb and I. "Taadaaa!" She took a bow, and her hair tumbled over her shoulders like a cape for a moment before she stood back up.

"What the fuck did you just do?" Tyb took a step back and leveled Vera at Aisha.

"Yeah, one of the things that kinda pissed me off about Christos, was that I got turned into a super-solider guinea pig. It's not that big of a deal." With a shrug of her shoulders, Aisha offered half a smile. "It is what it is."

"It's a very big deal, Aisha. Why would you let him do that? Mara said you consented, signed a waver or some shit."

"Mara only got half the story. I'm dying, Tyb. My neuropathy had gotten to the point where I couldn't function. I asked him if there was anything he could do. Turns out glittering skin, running up walls, thermo vision and the ability to make huge jumps are side effects. I don't feel pain any more, yay perk. But the whole wanting to gorge on blood… yeah. Not my cup of tea. Oh, and don't worry. I took out a couple deer before I got here, so I'm not so hungry right now." She smiled again.

Curious, I asked, "Wasn't the serum a part of a government project?"

She faced her brother while she spoke, her eyes never leaving Tyb's rifle. "Yeah, my 'cure' got parlayed as a weapon when the full scope of side effects made itself known."

I asked another question. "Why did he blow up the Berkeley lab?"

Aisha turned to me and spoke; her demeanor less bubbly. "Because he was angry. He didn't like his wife trying to play his game. So he rage quit."

Just like that, the epic temper tantrum that hobbled a state with fallout. Nice.

Tyb's voice was low. "Why are you here, Aisha?"

"Because I want your help in taking Christos out. He's fucking mental. And I know you hate his guts."

Tyb scoffed. "You were with him for years and you *just now* notice he's batshit crazy?"

"Yeah, well in all fairness, some reality checks take a little longer to cash than others. I was young and dumb, once. Just like you, Tyb. Do you want my help or not? Make up your mind; I'm getting tired of your inquisition. Oh, and who are you?" She addressed me.

"Sorry, Sis. But you've been gone for years, with a man you know tried killing me, and now you're back... I'll level with you. I'm suspicious."

"I'm Izzy."

"Yeah, hi Izzy. You know, you look a lot like Selesta Haytham. Fancy that, here in the backwoods. Didn't know you finally found someone, Tyb."

"You look a lot like Scarlet Johansson," I replied. And she really did, except her hair was a bit darker. Then again, wee hours of morning before dawn makes deciphering colors a bit on the difficult side. Aisha's heart-shaped face held two large eyes framed by trimmed brows. Her nose possessed an aquiline line, and her mouth, a perfect cupid's bow. I felt disorientated. Never thought I'd meet my husband's mistress. Didn't know how to act, so I'd just keep my mouth shut.

Tyb spoke up the moment Aisha opened her mouth to speak to me again. "Izzy and I have been exclusive how long now? A year?" I don't know why exactly he lied other than his distrust of Aisha, but I'd play his game.

"One year, two months and four days since we first spoke in that bar down the hill about animal husbandry. He swept me off my feet at the mention of goat groping and chasing flighty chickens."

"See? A woman after my own heart." Tyb wrapped an arm around me.

With oddly glowing eyes, Aisha stared me down. "Really. That long, eh? Didn't know barfly's were your style, Tov."

"Didn't know whack-ass nutjobs were your style, until it was too late, that is. What was it about him that made you tell everyone to fuck off so you could go live your little dream with his version of kinky fuckery?"

"Because I liked the pain. Made dealing with the neuropathy easier when I felt the hurt in other places. But I don't expect you to understand, just don't fuckin' judge, okay?" Suddenly she whirled around and peered between the tree-battlements, out into the forest next to the meadow. I could see her eyes glinting a bright lime green in the dark. It was unnatural and very unsettling. But not as unsettling as her next words. "He's coming."

Chapter Twenty-Eight

Tyb peered into the darkness with his night vision goggles, scanning the hills around us. "I don't see him, Aisha. How do you know he's close?"

"I can smell his cologne. No. 4711 is a very singular scent." Aisha pointed across the meadow and up the hill. "He's on the other side of that ridge."

Incredulous, I asked, "How can you smell him from here?"

Aisha turned her glowing eyes onto me. "Same reason I can see in the dark and jump really high. Because I'm special and you are not." She punctuated with a grin. "The serum didn't do anything for hearing, though."

"You can keep your special. I've got enough problems for now." I'd tell her she could keep Christos, too, but even she doesn't want him anymore.

"Fine, I will. And I won't even share. So there. Ha ha."

I found it hard to believe Zamara and Aisha were siblings, let alone twins. Day and night. Tyb spoke. "I want to know why you tried cutting Haytham, Little Sister."

She put her arms on hips and cocked an attitude. "Why is it any of your business, *Big Brother*?"

"Because I'm your favorite brother and I can't protect you if I don't have the whole story."

"You're my only brother, so that doesn't count. Don't protect me, Tybias Malcolm Dougherty. I am waaaay beyond your help. Was long ago, but just didn't know it."

"A- Do not call me by my full name, you are not Mom or Dad. B- If you are beyond help, why are you here?"

"To finish what Christ started seventeen years ago."

I jerked my rifle up and leveled at her. Didn't give Tyb a chance to respond. "Haytham tried killing Tyb back then. You here to finish that?" My finger moved the gun's safety to OFF. Tyb protected me. I'll protect him, even if it means shooting his glow-in-the-dark sister.

Aisha threw her head back and laughed. "No, silly mortal. You know how in chess, one player moves, then the other? Consider the clock broken for Tyb's move. Once upon a time, I loved Christos Haytham with every fiber of my being. I'd jump off a bridge if he said it'd make him happy… but then things change. He refused to marry me when I asked him a couple years back. Said at first he wanted to focus on his career. Ok, cool. Then he said I'm good enough to fuck, but not marry. Didn't want to ruin our relationship, didn't want that pressure. Didn't want to shackle himself to me because I can't have kids. And if I could, they'd be like me… a bloodthirsty freak because of that fucking serum. So he wooed some kid fresh out of college. Enchanted her enough to allow him to slip a ring on her finger, poor kid. She was the first chick who told him she didn't want to sign up for his BDSM fetish club … and so he married her. Bet she didn't know what lay ahead. That ring was a legal contract, he said. She signed the marriage license and that was just the same as signing his contract for sexy times. She didn't stand a chance."

I spoke, "I heard she and her bodyguard went over a cliff. It was all over the radio."

"Yeah. Christos was really upset. There went his reproduction plan. He's worse than a fucking Nazi with purity and shit. But I think it's a lie. I know if I were her, the first thing I'd want to do when I found out about the real him would to get the hell away. Maybe that's what she did. Anyhow, some crazy bitch sent Christos a text for a porn website. He freaked the fuck out because it's a private number. He said it was Selesta, taking revenge and how he couldn't allow her, or people pretending to be her make a fool of him."

Tyb spoke low, I guess to gauge her reaction. "Zamara was her bodyguard."

By the predawn light, I saw Aisha's face crumble at the realization her sister reportedly went over the cliff. "Have…have they found her?"

"Zamara is alive and well. She's been up here a couple times in the past month. Did Mara see you at the jail? She said she was heading your way to see you. In fact, she was the one who let me know you were arrested."

Aisha shook her head. "No, didn't see her. Maybe she'll come up here again. God, I missed her. She still married to Harry?"

"Hell no, they divorced years ago. She's happy flying single."

"I could learn a few things from her." Aisha spoke quietly.

Tyb nodded. "Yeah, we all can."

I took my eyes off the siblings and focused on the area Aisha gestured to earlier. "I think I can see him." Glowing green eyes were in the distance.

"If you can see him, he can see you, Izzy." Aisha's tone was that of a patient teacher explaining calculus to kindergarteners.

Tyb turned his head and watched Christos walk down the hill toward the meadow. "Aisha, you said you wanted to help take him out? Got any ideas?"

"Yeah I do. You won't like it, though. I'll channel my inner non-pedophilic Aunt MaryAnne."

"That means jackshit to me."

"His Aunt MaryAnne seduced and abused him when he was 15. I had a very enlightening conversation with her a while back and I think I found the key to getting my way with him. I want to do this, Tyb."

"You haven't told me anything, Aisha."

"Fine, you want to know? Here." She reached into the pocket of her jeans and pulled out a golfball sized hunk of something wrapped in plastic and handed it over to Tyb. "There you go. That's my idea."

He held it up and asked, "What's this? Putty? Going to sculpt him?"

"That's C-4, smartass. I'm gonna make him a buttplug. It'll be plug and play and boom. I even snatched a detonator, too."

Tyb almost dropped the explosive. "You're going to shove high explosives in his ass?"

With a wicked gleam, Aisha smiled. "That's the idea. Fucker will be fucked. Comeuppance. I…I should have walked away from him when he got married. Instead, I waited on the sideline, hoping he'd tell me it was a mistake; that it was me he should have married. But that never happened. Then she disappeared. And no matter what, he'd still never marry me. He'd still take his anger out on me as the price of him making the serum for me. I signed a lifetime long contract, that I was his. I'm ready to end that contract and keep him from being *him*. When he found out Selesta died, he told me all sorts of stuff he'd do to her. It wasn't sexy, it wasn't fun—at least not to her. He *tortured* that poor woman and called it *getting kinky*. I didn't do anything. I knew I could take the pain, but she didn't sign up for that. She wanted to just be married to that mask he wore. Mask fell off and she was left with a monster."

I spoke up, touched by what she said. "If he's that way, I doubt there was anything you could do to change him."

Her intense green eyes peered into my soul and said, "If you were me, what would you do? Let him rampage and inflict himself on others? He's already fucked Cali up enough that he ran to fucking Siberia to be safe while the high-intensity fallout settled elsewhere. Someone will have to kill him to stop him. I'm a fucking scientific vampire-zombie hybrid. Let's face it, I gotta die too before my implant completely fails. I'm as much a danger to people as he is."

Her words, true, and made me wonder just how much of a danger is she to Tyb?

Chapter Twenty-Nine

Aisha didn't continue the conversation. Christos had now reached the far edge of the meadow. She turned and leaped from the tree house's top to the middle of the field in a silent, single bound.

"Holy shit. Your sister has moves."

"Yeah, I know. And it scares the shit out of me."

Aisha now approached Christos. For a bit, quiet. Their words didn't carry to our ears until Christos demanded in a loud voice, "I want to know who *those* people are."

She responded just as loud. "That's my cousin, Brian, and his wife, Misha. I've imposed on them and so I'm going to see my parents."

Christos bellowed, "Don't you dare yell at me!"

"Don't *you* dare yell at *me*!" Aisha echoed his tone in perfect pitch.

Christos started stalking toward Tyb—er, *Brian*, and me, with Aisha following behind. I tried swallowing the knot growing in my throat. Tyb reached over and grasped my hand, interlocking his fingers between mine. "He cannot hurt you, *Misha*."

I grumbled under my breath, "You tell him that." Shifted my weight and watched Christos plowing through the meadow filled with waist-high spelt. Dawn started breaking, filling the forest with a soft light. "I so totally do not want to be here right now."

"If he needs reminding, I will do so. Repeatedly, until he understands no one lays a hand on you in anger. Take a deep breath. Remember, you are empowered. You are strong, you are armed. Remember what I said about guns and incapacitation?"

His words spoken months ago filled my mind. Gut shot, head shot. "Yeah. But it won't apply to them… they don't feel pain."

"Exactly. Aim for the head, especially in close quarters."

"If the saliva is infectious, could mean his blood is too. If we get sprayed by splatter…" my words drifted into silence. Oh shit, I wish I had asked Zamara about that possibility.

Tyb drew a deep breath. "Shit. I'm not comfortable trusting Aisha, especially with her history with him, but I don't see any other option. Fuckin' A, I hope we're not screwed."

"Fuck a B, it has two holes." I quieted as two sets of glowing green eyes looked up at Tyb and I from a dozen yards away.

Aisha did another great leap and landed near Tyb. Christos tried leaping, but couldn't get nearly the distance Aisha could. It was interesting to see him fail at something like that. Took four jumps for him to join us, and only one moment before I thought I was going to have a heart attack from being near Christos. But he gave no indication of noticing me. He appraised Tyb only, and noticed the guns we held with barrels to the sky, leaning against our shoulders; guns that look like they fell off the back of a military surplus truck.

Aisha spoke, "Christ, this is my cousin, Brian O'Mara, and his wife, Misha."

She kept calling him Christ and it made me think of when I asked him why I couldn't call him Chris. Because he was twice as Christ-like as anyone, he said. *Shudder.*

"You already told me that, Aisha." He addressed Tyb in a very rude manner, "Why you have guns? Always greet your cousin this way?"

"Regular twenty-one gun salute, for long-lost cousin Aisha. Actually, we're waiting for dawn to hit. Deer will be out to graze. Venison is about as close I can get to heaven up in the mountains. Backstrap is a truly splendid thing. Ever had it? Want to try it?"

It blew me away how congenial Tyb seemed to be toward Christos. Aisha's and my own eyes met in a silent look that conveyed both our expectation that the other boot would drop soon.

"Never ate deer. Seems barbaric."

Tyb cleared his throat and asked, "Vegan?"

"No. Just not a savage who must kill woodland creatures." Christos looked around, very *not* impressed with the cement behemoth he stood upon.

And since when did Christos give a fuck about animals?

"Kinder to hunt than let starvation and disease kill them during winter."

"True, I suppose…"

"Well, Christos. Let's get going. Got a long hike back down to the road." Aisha put her arm through his and tried leading him away.

"You know, Aisha my sweet," It curdled my blood to hear him call her that. Just creepy with his tone which seemed to hint toward dark intentions. "I *am rather* hungry, but we're on that *special* diet…"

She put a hand on his forearm. "Then let's go somewhere *else* to eat. It'll be too much of a hassle to bother Brian, especially since we interrupted their hunting."

"We will stay, Aisha." His voice became that domineering tone which used to cow me. Now I was just getting irked.

Evidently his tone pissed Aisha off. A look crossed her face and settled into a stern case of cold bitch. "*We will not.* Let's go *now.*"

He shook her arm off and I stepped closer to Tyb. Christos spat, "Do not talk to me, bitch."

Clear as the dawn sky, Aisha spoke, "*Mulier est hominis crudelius.*"

Woman is crueler than man.

Christos fell to his knees, a look of wonder on his face, a look that bespoke an apostle looking upon his savior. Then he remembered himself. Downcast his eyes, and prostrated himself before Aisha. "My queen, what is your pleasure?"

She kicked him in the side. "You will apologize for imposing on my beloved family. That was not well done, *peon.*"

I looked at Aisha and when I had her gaze, I mouthed, *How?* How can four words have my ex abuser on the ground, accepting a woman's domination? Blew my mind.

Aisha mouthed, *MaryAnne.* That talk… must have been about Christos' training.

Still on his knees, Christos turned around, head down, and said, "Forgive me, I was rude."

"Aisha, you can let him up now." I could tell by the amused look trying to hide on Tyb's face that he was as blown away as I.

"Do you hear that, peon? You have pleased the master of this land. You may arise. I will reward you for behaving."

Christos arose and kept his head down. "Thank you, my queen."

"Brian, can I take Christos up to the house and scrounge around? It's been a long hike."

Tyb hesitated a minute. "Sure."

Aisha took a mighty leap, covering at least 100 feet. She yelled,*"Mulier…..!"*

In a heartbeat, Christos scrambled to clear the faux-tree battlements and join his mistress. She waited while he bounded about 15 leaps to catch up to Aisha's position. He cocked an arm, which she took, and they ambled at a sedate pace toward the house.

"What the fuck just happened?" I asked to no one in particular.

"I…fuck, I got not idea."

"Christos was groomed as a kid by his pedophile next door neighbor. She abused him for years. I think Aisha got some lessons from MaryAnne on how to bring him to heel."

Tyb nodded, and I noticed how the golden light highlighted his dark hair. "My sister scares me."

Well, yeah. She scares me too. "If they are going to the house, think the passports and stuff should be moved here from the panic room? Especially if there's going to be an explosive sex toy involved?"

"That's a good idea. Let's go inside, lock up. You'll stay here while I run and get some stuff. I won't be long, maybe 15 minutes, especially at the pace their going."

With that, we rushed inside, no telling how long we really have before things get all adventurous and stuff. We walked back to the room with the table and sink. I sat down at the table and Tyb opened the door to the tunnel and began jogging.

I waited in the most painful silence when his footfalls quieted. If Aisha was going to do as she said, then... what? Tyb's house will be gone. His sister. She's willing to sacrifice herself to keep Christos from doing further harm. Isolated up on the mountain, we're far away from the reality of the terror in the bay area. Tyb told me that the Round Valley area we were in was actually a naturally-formed fallout shelter secreted by the government. Fuck, and being so close to Christos and him not realizing it was me... was on the verge of freaking out. Lost in thought, Tyb was setting stuff on the table when I got jerked back to reality. I looked up and noticed he'd already shut the door.

"I locked the gun safe, got the passports and other stuff here, and this," Tyb began removing a belt I didn't notice. I looked around him and noted the belt was attached to a large, misshapen sack by a stout length of rope.

"What's that?" Curiosity soaked through me.

He grinned. "My pirate's booty."

"You have a big booty."

"Thanks for noticing."

He bent down and unzipped the sack. My jaw dropped when I saw a fortune in gold nuggets. "Holy fucking cow. Gold panning?"

"Yep. Kept two pounds for every year I went. So that's twenty pounds and something like over half a mil. Some of it is yours. I didn't get to take you panning, and I want to make sure you're not lacking once you get back to civilization.

Tyb stood up and joined me at the table. "I, uh, just want you to know, Izzy, that I wish you could stay up here. I've enjoyed your company very much." His warm amber eyes looked into mine and I was about to speak when he continued. "You're a very special lady. Never forget it."

With the tone he used, oh, I won't forget it. "You're an incredibly awesome guy, Tyb. I envy the woman who finally tames you."

My statement was punctuated by a huge boom which rocked the earth and shattered our world.

Chapter Thirty

Fire engulfed the hill where Tyb's home once stood. The sound of everything cracking as it burnt filled the sky like smoke. We stood in the meadow so we could see the house off in the distance. Our guns, slung over our shoulders. We stood in awe of repeated blasts rocked the forest, the shockwave for each rapport trembling the earth.

"Fuuuuuuck. I forgot about the dynamite." Arms were at his side, his face impassive.

"What?" We stood outside, watching flames swallow and shatter and smoke.

"Left over from building... there were some huge boulders I had to remove to lay foundation. They...well, if the C-4 didn't do him in..." His voice trailed off and I bet he was thinking of his little sister. I know I was.

My suspicions were confirmed when Tyb fell to his knees and his eyes brimmed with tears. The firelight glistened with the yet-unshed emotion. The man who has always seemed so strong to me, so assured and competent, now reduced to a man shattered by tragedy. He wanted nothing more than to save his sister from Christos Haytham. Now she died with Christos Haytham. She died because she felt bad for Selesta, *me*. Dammit. This isn't how life is supposed to be. Happy endings, how passé are they nowadays? I felt nothing for Christos other than relief. "Dammit, Tyb. I am so sorry."

I sat down beside him and wrapped him in my arms. Felt him shaking and shuddering with emotion.

"She ran away once, she ran away twice. But now she'll never come back." Tyb's voice was more steady that my own.

"She loved you. She protected you from him. She is so

very brave." The bravest person I know.

"I should have protected her. Science could have saved her…"

"Or she could have attacked us when her implant completely fails. That was a possibility. Nothing will make you feel better, Tyb, except for time. I wish I could say something that would make everything make sense. I don't have that super power."

He drew a deep breath, and with a focus I envied, seemed to center himself and find his calm. "We survived the zompire apocalypse. Want to know the dream?"

Distraction from his pain. I could respect that. "Please."

"I dreamed the house was in flames. It's why I put the IDs in the panic room. Fire and death. I didn't know it was going to be Aisha. I thought it was going to be me… Never Aisha. Not until she put that chunk of C-4 in my hand." Tyb turned his face to mine and my heart crumbled with the anguish evident, etched deep in his eyes. "You're free, Izzy. You can leave Selesta to rest in peace, or you can resurrect her. Could cash in on whatever is left of Haytham's estate, live a very comfortable life. Do whatever you want."

I swallowed the lump in my throat. "I really don't want to leave the mountain, not if it means I never see you again. I agree, my family needs to see me and know I'm fine… but I…" I didn't know how to continue without revealing too much of myself and face rejection. "I hope our paths cross again, Tyb. Soon."

Tyb reached out and covered my hand with his own, then gave a gentle squeeze. "The future is not writ in stone. And if it were, time would erase it away." He leaned over and kissed me on the forehead with cool lips.

I couldn't hold the tears in anymore. Everything crashed around me, the sense of aimlessly adrift in life. And death. Goddamn, the death.

"I love you Tyb."

"Not as much as I love you. I love you enough that I know I need to let you go." He stood up and began walking back to the treehouse.

I sat in the meadow, now awash with morning sunlight

streaming through copious smoke, weeping. It shouldn't be a surprise, he told me time and again not to love him, not to care. He never led me on. The hurt I feel in regards to the prospect I nurtured of Tyb and I together, it'd pass, eventually. He taught me a great many things I needed to know.

I heard sounds of scratching from the far side of the treehouse. I got up to investigate, lifting my teeshirt hem up to blot my eyes. As I walked around the other side of the cement fortress, I saw something horrible. A naked body, most of the flesh burnt off, one arm and a part of the chest cavity missing. Gore hung like old lace. His back faced me, and I could see him convulsing, revealing what was left of his face and what was causing the jerking.

Christos. Missing his lower jaw.

He had Tyb in a chokehold with his one arm, while Tyb tried throwing him off balance.

Christos spoke, but it sounded "Sthand sthill, dan you! Thith will only thake a moment."

Tyb fought, but it seemed that Christos never tired of the wrestling. With his attention focused on Tyb, he didn't notice me creeping up behind him, my rifle at the ready, finger caressing the trigger. Oh, if he fucking hurts Tyb…

My barrel was six inches away from the back of Christos' skull when Tyb played dead weight and was dropped. As soon as Tyb's head was out of the way, I fired. When Tyb heard the first shot, he rolled out of the way.

Semi-Automatic. Every time I pulled the trigger, another round made its way to visit the wonderland of Christos' Synapses. I emptied my clip into my undead ex-husband, until there was nothing left of his head but a bloody stump.

His carcass fell to the ground.

I dropped the rifle and plopped onto my knees. Fuck. I just kill, er, rekilled someone. Head shot, just like Tyb said.

"You okay, Izzy?" His arms wrapped around me and I buried my face in the crook of his neck. This man is my happy place.

"Yeah. I think I am."

The sound of quads filled the mountain air. At the lead,

Mara. Everyone parked in the middle of the meadow and I couldn't help thinking, *there goes the harvest this year.*

"What happened?" She vaulted off the quad and bounded toward us. She stopped short when she saw what was left of Haytham. Her eyes widened and took in Tyb and I. Peeling myself away from him, I asked, "Is blood as contagious as the saliva?" I needed to know, now that I was covered in Christos' A positive.

"No, just the saliva. The enzymes which break up carbs is what triggers the whole chain reaction."

I breathed a massive sigh of relief.

Mara's comrades surrounded us and she spoke. "We need to get you guys out of here for decontamination and debriefing." Two officers lead Tyb and I in different directions, asking questions regarding what happened.

It was the last time I saw Tyb.

Mara said my contact would meet me at the bar on Mill Avenue.

Tempe is not my first choice when it comes to selecting a place for relocation. But monsoon season was upon us, and that helped make the Arizona heat a bit more bearable.

The bar was fairly non-descript. A couple bull's-eyes for darts hung on a well-perforated wall. Smoke from cigarettes hung in the air while I nursed a rum and coke.

Mara. She called one day, out of the blue. Asked if I had time to help her with a project. With life being boring at the moment, her offer was the spice I needed. My contact would be a male going by the name of Iain St. Cloud.

This wasn't the first time I helped her. Been three years since I left the mountain. About six months after my relocation, Mara asked if I could pick up a package for her from a locker. No prob. I also listened to an offer made by another contact and relayed it back to her. I placed bugs in restaurants known to be frequented by Russian mafia. Shits and giggles.

I love working for the University of Arizona's library. Not head librarian, but I'm damn good at research. But research amidst books can be dull after a while.

Selesta stayed dead. I visited my parents and let them know the whole story—well, not all the Tyb parts. I am Izabeau D'Beafort, now. Single as the day is long. My cat and I share an apartment. I named her Aisha.

I sat in a back booth, positioned so I could see who comes through the bar's door. He's supposed to be here by eight-thirty. If not by nine, I'm supposed to leave. Can do. Listen to his offer and report back. In the meanwhile, enjoy my time with Captain

Morgan.

At eight-forty-five, a tall man carrying a briefcase strode through the glass door and looked around. Couldn't see his face under the cowboy hat—and Arizona has a lot of cowboy hat-wearing folks. His head turned my way, and he walked over. Jeans and a black tee-shirt covered his frame.

"Izabeau?"

I nodded my head. "Mr. St. Cloud?"

His voice was deep, tingle-inducing. "A Ms. Malone is an acquaintance of yours, correct?"

"That is correct." The dim bar made it hard to make out the contours of the man's face. "Will you join me?"

"Don't mind if I do." He laid the briefcase on the table and sat opposite me. Didn't take off the hat, just kept it tilted down, shielding his face.

"Ms. Malone said you had an offer to make…?"

"Yes. This offer is for you."

"Me?" This isn't how it's supposed to work. He makes offer, I relay message. That is all.

"Yes, you."

"May I see your face? I like to know who I'm talking to."

"Certainly." He doffed his hat and my jaw dropped.

"Tyb?"

He smiled at me. "Hi you."

"Why the act?"

"Didn't know how you felt about me."

I still fucking love him. Lay awake at night and relive the memories of being alone with him, secluded from the world in a paradise of his own creation.

"I don't have any negative feelings, if that's what you're asking." But now I'm way confused.

"Are… are you seeing anyone?"

I smiled, blown away by this strange quirk of life. "Nope."

"Me either."

"So did you really have an offer, or was this an elaborate set up just to have drinks and catch up?"

"There's an offer I wanted to make you."

He opened up the briefcase and showed me the contents. "You forgot this when you left."

Hundred dollar bills in tidy stacks, banded together with a very official strip of paper. "What? I don't understand."

"From the gold. This was your cut."

"Wow. I don't know what to say. Thank you. You don't need to, though."

"I know. But for three years I've sat on it. I want you to have it."

"What happened to your homestead?"

"I had to move, per big brother."

"That sucks. I loved it up there."

"So did I. Now I'm in Yuma. Got a business going."

"Oh, do tell." I was curious how Tyb reconciled his wilderness man to city living.

"I run a farming-coop and live in a modified earthship. I was uh, wondering if you were considering a change in career. I could use a partner."

"I don't know anything about running a business, Tyb."

"The position I had in mind was more of the girlfriend kind." His eyes looked upon me, expectantly.

My heart swelled. He was right, that dawn three years ago. Nothing is writ in stone that time cannot change. "I think I would like that."

A TOAST TO STARRY NIGHTS

Chapter One

How does one deal with such a disastrous scenario? Here I was, dressed to the nines, and here he was on bended knee, ring in hand and covered in my regurgitated dinner. Dignity wasn't an option-- all tables around us were staring, whispering, or choking back the puke themselves. Was it the smell, sight or sound that set them off? Just one glance around and I saw all eyes were on us, and characteristically, I ruined a beautiful moment by doing the wrong thing. I always got queasy when anxious, and right now, being center stage, made me extremely nervous.

Snow-white linen and crystal chandeliers faded into the background as I looked upon my boyfriend of four years before me as I sat at the center-most table in the restaurant. I was more than aware of every pair of eyes focused on the tableau he and I provided as an aperitif.

Dmitri was frozen on his knee, mouth agape. A lock of dark brown hair fell from its gelled haven onto his forehead. His best suit jacket was covered in prime rib, creamed spinach, wine and bile. I couldn't help but to think that I needed to pay for the dry cleaning, give him a back massage, and my undying gratitude for not throwing up on me in return-- I saw him hold back a heave with a shudder.

By some miracle, my bomb missed his trouser leg altogether. "I'm sorry. Please get me out of here," I whispered. I hated being the center of attention and curiosity, upset that I made a scene and completely destroyed such lovely intentions. The tears were welling up and I had no desire to make a horrendous scene worse.

"Are you okay?" he asked, concern heavy in his accented voice. I watched as a piece of red meat slid down his dark gray jacket and the urge to pass out flashed through my mind as it plopped onto the floor.

"I just threw up on you..." Perhaps he couldn't see my Captain Obvious cape fluttering in the imaginary breeze. My eyes closed and I gripped the edge of the table as the new bout of nausea wound its way up from the twisting innards that couldn't be mentally tamed. My words must have assured him I wouldn't expire on the spot.

Dmitri smiled wryly and replied, "Yeah, I noticed." He stood up and peeled off the offensive garment. With great care he folded it inside out to make a neat bundle out of the purple silk-lined jacket. "I'm going to pay the bill, why don't you head out to the car? I'll meet you there in a few." Dmitri winked at me, trying to elicit a smile.

It didn't work. I lacked the gumption. If only I could fade from view and slip out unnoticed. I needed to master that particular trick and channel my inner ninja.

As an afterthought, I looked down to my periwinkle blue dress and saw I missed decorating myself in regurgitation. Although it seemed repugnant, at that moment I wish I had covered myself in upchuck instead of the man who wanted me as his wife. I could easily bear self-humiliation if it meant giving Dmitri all his dignity back. That he could be so cool and collected after getting coated in dinner earned him more admiration from me.

A waiter in a penguin suit stood off to one side, signaling the bus boy to clean up. I guess he was wondering if I'd heave chunks on him too. My wine glass was still half-full

of a rather decent Syrah, which I chugged in a most
unladylike manner. Already have everyone's attention,
might as well seal the deal for lowbrow dining at a quality
establishment by guzzling my grape juice like an
over-enthusiastic sorority pledge. Didn't care anymore, I
already ruined the night.

Wine helped to rid my mouth of the astringent taste of bile.
Standing up, I gathered my belongings and apologized to
the waiter. I dug briefly into my purse and pulled out two
twenty dollar bills. Were I in his shoes, an apology and
good tip would be a very nice thing indeed.

Through the crowded dining room and out the exit, past
burning stares and loud whispers, I made my escape.
Caught sight of myself in a mirror behind the maitre'd
station. My hazel eyes looked like twin pissholes in the
snow. Out the etched plate-glass door and into the parking
lot I went. The summer night had a gentle rose-scented
breeze, which helped to clear my head, and the lingering
nausea abate. Upon reaching the car, I realized that Dmitri
locked it and still possessed the keys. As I waited, I rested
my head atop my arms crossed on the Jetta and pondered
why I would do such a thing at an important moment in my
life.

I had expected Dmitri's proposal ever since my mother
dropped broad hints a few months ago. The reality of the
moment was so much better than anything I could imagine,
with the exception of my oral eruption. My own version
of Pompeii, except Dmitri was the only one smothered by
the lava flow. Sigh. The giddiness of the moment may have
played into it. The crowd of people staring didn't really
help. But there was a stabbing moment of sheer panic and
abject fright that I couldn't place as he offered the ring to
me with such pride and love shining in his wonderful bright

blue eyes. I loved the idea of getting married to Dmitri yet
the thought of the wedding itself didn't sit well with me. It
was the first time I ever felt true fear in the presence of
Dmitri, yet it wasn't he I feared, but the nuptial ceremony.
The thought niggled my mind in a way that let me feeling
bewildered and apprehensive.

Footsteps sounded his approach. I raised my head, not
caring that my elaborate hairstyle came undone and dark
red curls hung in clumps to my shoulders. Every time I
closed my eyes to blink, that one moment replayed itself
in my mind. How could I look at him now?

There was no need for me to fret. Dmitri gathered me into
his arms and rested his chin upon the crown of my head.
Surely stray hairpins were sticking into him, but he seemed
not to care.

"Honestly now, Kaylis, are you okay?"

"I...I don't know. I mean, yes, I want to marry you, but I
don't know why I threw up. I'm so sorry, Dmitri. I didn't
mean to ruin your proposal." *In front of all of Chico,* I
silently amended.

"Kay, the only way you'd ruin it is if you said no."

Somewhere in my rib cage, my heart began to thaw from its
frozen state of fear. He took a step away from me, and I felt
bereft of his presence. He reached into his pant pocket and
drew out the box he had already offered me once. Now
with my stomach devoid of any content, I suppose he felt
safe in offering it to me again.

With slow grace, he unhinged the tiny rosewood cube,
carved with ivy and flowers by his own hands. "Kaylis

Woods, would you do me the honor of becoming my wife?"
Even in the dark, the blue of his eyes shone bright. With a
smile, Dmitri proffered the ring nestled inside the wooden
sculpture to me.

"Yes." I didn't know what else to say, although wrapping
my arms around him and squeezing with all my might did
cross my mind as a more dignified version of an intense
girly-moment-squeal-of-delight.

He slid the ring onto my finger and I studied it for a brief
moment. A large cobalt-blue square-cut sapphire had a
marquise diamond set on each side, at the midpoint. Filling
in the spaces between the diamonds were tiny round iolites
in a watery lavender-blue color. The band was filigreed
platinum, pierced so that light could shine through to the
stones and make them sparkle with an inner fire.

Dmitri now held my fingertips prisoner in his gentle grasp.
As I marveled at the magnitude of his gift, his voice
caressed my ear. "The jeweler thought that the diamonds
should have been mounted at each point of the sapphire.
But I wanted them right where they are, at the compass
points. I lived a life without you before, Kaylis. I felt lost.
When I am with you, I know exactly where I am, and
where I want to be. You are my compass and so I am lost
no more. You are very special to me."

My heart puddled at his poetry, and as fast as an Oklahoma
twister, I whipped around and wrapped my arms about his
neck and kissed the side of his mouth-- he wasn't going to
get a full-on kiss until I had brushed my teeth. "You are
mine, as I am yours," I whispered.

At my passionate decree, I felt the terror re-emerge in the
pit of my stomach, and I closed my eyes as it unfurled. I

hugged Dmitri again, using the strength and warmth of his embrace as my shield against the unexplained and unreasonable icy-cold terror. His breath tickled my neck to sweep the fear away.

No more than a moment had passed, and Dmitri was unaware of my silent mini panic attack. I basked in the love of this man and whispered, "You are ten kinds of awesome." Dmitri returned my hug and swung me around underneath the glowing halo of parking lot lights. We laughed and my personal Pompeii lay forgotten in our shared happiness.

AVAILABLE IN PRINT AND ON KINDLE

About the Author

Mandi Rei Serra

Raised in Northern California as a middle child (and only girl) she devoured books as soon as she could heft them from the book shelf.

Been all over the western half of the United States, absorbing knowledge from the little enclaves of culture. It's amazing what 50 miles can do to change the mindset of people. Amazing.

Now a thirty-something geek penning homage to all sorts of nifty things and raising two minions to do her bidding.

Anthropology, History, Geology, Theology, Psychology and weird stuff garner her interest pretty quickly. Quirkier, the better.

She loves hearing from readers!
Mandi Rei's website www.MandiReiSerra.com and for the Tweeps, www.twitter.com/MandiReiSerra

Mandi Rei Serra's erotica-writing alter ego: Alana Twincannon's blog for updates and saucy snippets: www.tawdryerotica.blogspot.com and on Twitter @AlanaTwincannon